"May I come i[n]?"
Carlos asked

"I—we have nothing to say to each other...Mr. Hastings," she stammered.

"I think we have," he persisted, and as she tried to close the door, he put the flat of his hand against it.

Her temper flared. "How dare you force your way in here?"

"I haven't forced my way in, yet. I am merely preventing you from slamming the door in my face," he answered smoothly.

"You are deceitful," she said, staring into his dark Spanish eyes.

"And you are a liar." His face was suddenly taut with angry contempt. She had seen Carlos Hastings in several moods, but now the mask of amused charm was off, revealing the face of a man with a much fiercer temper than hers. And the wide sensual mouth that had kissed her was set in a punitive line.

ANNE WEALE is one of Harlequin's busiest writers—and also one of the most traveled. She gave up her original career as a journalist to follow her husband to the Far East. British citizens by birth, Anne and her husband have lived for the past five years in a Spanish villa high above the Mediterranean. They have traveled extensively researching new romantic backgrounds—New England, Florida, the Caribbean, Italy—and their latest journeys have taken them through Canada to Australia and the Pacific. Swimming, interior decorating, antique hunting and needlepoint are among Anne's many interests.

Books by Anne Weale

ANTIGUA KISS
FLORA
SUMMER'S AWAKENING

HARLEQUIN PRESENTS

HARLEQUIN ROMANCE

Don't miss any of our special offers. Write to us at the following address for information on our newest releases.

Harlequin Reader Service
901 Fuhrmann Blvd., P.O. Box 1397, Buffalo, NY 14240
Canadian address: P.O. Box 603,
Fort Erie, Ont. L2A 5X3

ANNE WEALE

night train

Harlequin Books

TORONTO • NEW YORK • LONDON
AMSTERDAM • PARIS • SYDNEY • HAMBURG
STOCKHOLM • ATHENS • TOKYO • MILAN

Harlequin Presents first edition March 1988
ISBN 0-373-11061-8

Original hardcover edition published in 1987
by Mills & Boon Limited

CHAPTER ONE

SARAH was halfway down the flight of stairs between the hall and the first floor of her employers' London house when she heard a key turning in the lock of the front door. Expecting to see Tim Ardsley who six months ago, with his wife, had engaged her to look after their infant son Alexander, she began to smile a friendly welcome as the door was pushed open.

But it wasn't Alexander's father who stepped into the hall and rubbed the soles of his shoes on the large sunken doormat. It was a much taller man, who didn't immediately notice the slender, fair-haired girl coming down the staircase.

When Sarah saw who it was, she stopped short, her grey eyes widening in shock recognition of someone she hadn't seen for a year and, during that time, had done her best to forget.

Following him into the hall, Tim Ardsley closed the panelled door topped by an elegant Regency fanlight. 'Let me take your coat, Hastings.'

'Thank you.' The tall black-haired man with the unseasonably sun-tanned face unwound a cashmere scarf and shrugged off his navy blue coat. His suit was also navy blue, chalk-striped, superbly cut—or would his broad-shouldered athletic frame have made any suit look good?

In the short time Sarah had known him, he had worn casual hot-weather clothes. This Englishman-about-town persona was a side of him unfamiliar to her.

Tim caught sight of her standing, frozen, on the beige-carpeted stairs, gripping the gleaming mahogany hand-rail.

'Hello, Sarah. Are you going out? I'd have kept our taxi if I'd realised. The rain's belting down. You'll have to call a radio cab. Can't stand on the corner on a night like this—you'd get drenched.'

The house was in Albion Street, a quiet one-way road off the busy thoroughfare along the north side of Hyde Park. The corner to which Tim was referring was the junction of Albion Street and Connaught Street which, with its fishmonger, chemist, flower shop, restaurant, pub, pet shop, hairdressers and newsagent, seemed more like the main street of a village or small country town than a segment of a huge metropolis only a few minutes' walk from the vortex of day and night traffic swirling around Marble Arch.

The man with Tim Ardsley looked up and stared at the girl on the staircase. If he recognised her, he gave no sign of it. Perhaps he didn't. A year was a long time in the life of an eligible bachelor with the looks and the means to attract almost any woman who caught his wandering fancy.

Tim introduced her. 'This is Sarah Lancaster, my son's nanny.' Although usually he treated Sarah with every courtesy, he didn't complete the introduction by telling her who his guest was.

The taller man inclined his head. 'How do you do, Miss Lancaster.' Not for the first time, his dark eyes appraised her small-waisted figure and slim legs.

When she had met him, in Spain, she had been wearing white trousers with a cotton Fair Isle sweater in her favourite shades of turquoise and apricot, and a pair of cheap but fun ear-rings bought from a stall in the market at Algeciras.

Tonight there were pearls in her ears and a thermal

camisole under her cream silk shirt with its big padded shoulders. A narrow black skirt, black lace tights and high-heeled black patent pumps completed her outfit for dinner *à quatre* at a popular Kensington restaurant. Her hair, still shoulder-length but no longer the curly mane it had been last spring at Sotogrande, was brushed smoothly back from her forehead and held by a black velvet Alice band.

'How do you do,' she answered stiffly, as if to a stranger—except that with strangers her manner was usually warm and open.

She wondered how Tim would react if he knew that she and this man he had brought home had once been forced by exigency to share a sleeping compartment on a crowded night train from Algeciras to Madrid. The memory of that journey across Spain and France to Paris, where they had parted, would haunt her for the rest of her life. At the outset she had been wary of him, or told herself that she was. At the end, by the time they reached Paris . . .

Her mind shied from recollections she had been at pains to suppress in the long twelve months since their final glimpse of each other at the Gare d'Austerlitz, the station in Paris where passengers on the motorail collected their cars and went their separate ways.

With more presence of mind than his host, Carlos Hastings said, 'The taxi may not have gone yet,' and quickly re-opened the door to peer into the street which, as usual, had both its pavements lined with parked cars.

Invariably these included several Rolls-Royces, and every time she passed one of the opulent vehicles on her way to the park with Alexander, Sarah thought what a crazy world it was in which people paid hundreds of thousands of pounds for houses which had no garages, and tens of thousands on cars which had to be left in the street where any passing hooligan could scratch their expensive paintwork.

To a country-bred girl imbued with the conservative values of a family whose eldest sons had for generations served their country in the Army before retiring to a small and increasingly shabby manor house, the extravagant ways of the residents of Albion Street—and of the man in the doorway—were a source of wonder and amazement.

Luckily the taxi had not yet moved off. Grabbing an umbrella from the stand inside the front door but not pausing to open it, Carlos Hastings dashed into the rain to prevent the cab's departure.

Sarah barely had time to put on her raincoat before he was back, the umbrella unfurled, with the obvious intention of holding it over her between the house and the taxi. To give the devil his due—and he was the most devilish man she had ever encountered—he had always had impeccable manners.

'Please don't bother . . . I have an umbrella,' she said, unbuttoning the cover on a folding red one.

'No need to open that now.' Grasping her by the elbow, he hustled her through the downpour to the waiting cab. 'Where to?' he asked, releasing her arm to open the door for her.

'Clarke's restaurant in Kensington Church Street, please.'

Still holding open the rear door, he repeated the address to the driver. Then he looked in at Sarah and she felt sure he *had* recognised her and thought he was going to say something. But after a long intent stare, he said only, 'Enjoy yourself,' and shut the door and turned away towards the house where Tim Ardsley was waiting for him.

Sarah sank back against the smooth leather upholstery, still feeling the masterful grip of his long brown fingers on her elbow. She could also feel her heart beating in agitated thumps and her hands were shaking. Would she be able to pull herself together in the short time it would take to reach the restaurant? Somehow she must.

If only she had left the house ten minutes earlier this wouldn't have happened; they wouldn't have met again. Their brief encounter would still be an unhappy memory which most of the time she managed to keep locked away in a sort of mental boxroom with another distressing recollection, the loss of her mother.

As the taxi swung into Bayswater Road, passing the Park's ornate railings which every Sunday were hung with the paintings of numerous hopeful artists, Sarah made a strong effort to put out of her mind the shattering *rencontre* which had just taken place.

It was impossible. No effort of will would dismiss Carlos Hastings' compelling dark face from her mind. Indeed, as the taxi sped westward and the street lamps illuminated the rain driving down through the budding branches of the trees lining the wet roadway, she found herself remembering the brilliantly hot morning of her arrival at Málaga airport, where she had first set eyes on him.

'Carlos! Qué sorpresa!'

The strikingly beautiful Spanish girl who had sat near Sarah on the aeroplane seemed surprised at being met by the man who dipped his tall head to kiss her lightly on both cheeks.

He was as good-looking as the girl, with a palpable charm which, although it was focused on the lovely brunette, also had an effect on the fair English girl who had followed her through Customs into the public concourse.

For a few moments Sarah forgot to look around for her grandmother, who was meeting her, and instead watched the debonair Spaniard relieving the girl of her hand luggage.

An expensive suitcase and a large carrier with *Harrods* printed on the side of it were in the charge of a porter waiting nearby. He could probably tell from their conversation what their relationship was. Sarah, who spoke a little Spanish but not nearly enough to understand the girl's rapid chatter, had no way of knowing what they were to each other.

Brother and sister? The disparity in their ages—she was younger than Sarah, he looked about thirty-five—didn't rule out that relationship, but her reaction to him did. A sister wouldn't sparkle like that for an older brother. If they were related, it was at a distance which permitted her to be attracted to him.

And he was the kind of man to whom, in purely physical terms, almost any female would feel some degree of attraction. Not only because he was many inches taller than the average Spaniard, with shoulders in proportion to his height and muscles where other men had flab. A man could be tall and deep-chested with powerful arms and long hard thighs, but the face which went with those attributes could cancel them out.

This man hadn't *that* kind of face. His features were as well-proportioned as his limbs. A strong chin. An aquiline nose. Dark Andalusian eyes deep-set under mobile black eyebrows.

But it was the air of the man, as much as his tall lithe frame and fine profile, which caught and held attention. He looked as if nothing would daunt him; as if, no matter what happened, he would always know what to do. Perhaps it was an illusion, but that was the impression he gave, and it was that total self-

confidence, allied to his physical assets, which gave
him outstanding presence.

'Sarah . . . my dearest child . . . how lovely to
see you!'

The familiar voice of her grandmother roused Sarah
from her somewhat mesmerised interest in the Spanish
couple and made her pale face light up as she turned
to greet Molly Grantham.

Mrs Grantham was in her seventies, but still slim
and active. Unlike Sarah, whose pallor was the result
of the long, cold, wet spring in England, her grandmother was nut-brown from her deeply lined, smiling
face to her bare legs and sandalled feet.

'Granny! How are you?' Sarah set down her suitcase
to hug with both arms the woman with whom she
shared a special bond, her mother's mother.

'I only just made it in time,' said Mrs Grantham
when, a few minutes later, they were walking out of
the airport. 'The traffic between here and Marbella
gets worse every year. It's impossible now to remember
what this coast was like years ago when Robert and I
first came down here. But it's still not too bad at my
end, thank goodness. In fact you may find it too quiet.
Most of the apartments are empty and I don't think
the hotel has many people staying there at present.
The season hasn't really begun yet.'

'I haven't come for a social whirl. All I want to do
is to soak up some sun and sort out my future,' said
Sarah, giving a sigh of pleasure at the warmth and
brilliance of the weather here compared with the chilly
morning she had left behind her.

She had set out from home wearing a padded gilet
over a cowl-necked sweater over a cotton shirt. Now
she was carrying the gilet and, after dumping her
suitcase in the back of her grandmother's car, she
pulled off the sweater and started rolling up her shirt

sleeves. As she did so a silver sports car glided into
the aisle where she was standing, her hair still in
disorder after the removal of the sweater.

It was a Porsche 928, the car of her younger
brother's dreams, with a price to match its speed,
power and cachet. Not altogether surprisingly, the
man at the wheel was the tall Spaniard called Carlos.
As he cruised past on his way to the exit, he gave
Sarah a cursory glance. For perhaps two seconds, no
more, their eyes met, leaving her with the deflating
feeling that, while he was unquestionably the most
attractive man she had ever seen, she had made as
much impression on him as one of the concrete pillars
supporting the shade-roof above the line of parked
cars.

Sarah had no illusions about her looks. She wasn't
a beauty like her mother, but neither was she a plain
girl, accustomed to masculine indifference. No man,
to her recollection, had ever looked *through* her rather
than at her before. It was a most disconcerting experience, particularly coming from someone who had
made a strong impact on her.

There must have been some delay at the pay booth,
because the silver Porsche was still in the queue when
her grandmother's Ford Fiesta joined the line of cars
waiting to leave. When, a few minutes later, the
Porsche swung out of the car park, Sarah saw with
surprise that it had a British number plate. How very
odd, she thought, hearing the deep-throated boom as
it gathered speed and disappeared. What was a
Spaniard doing with a car registered in Britain?

Puzzling about it reminded her that, at the end of
her holiday, she would be taking back to England her
grandfather's British-registered, right-hand-drive
Lancia.

After Robert Grantham's sudden death, a little

more than a year ago, many of Molly Grantham's relations and friends had expected her to return to her own country. But she, accustomed for years to the more benign climate of her adopted homeland, had preferred to remain in Andalusia, albeit with modifications to her lifestyle.

Since Sarah's last visit, her grandmother had moved from a rather isolated farmhouse in the foothills of the Sierra Bermeja to a garden flat at Sotogrande, a luxury development catering to rich Americans and élite Madrileñas who, when Madrid sweltered in the intolerable heat of August, escaped to their holiday houses on the coast of Andalusia, accompanied by retinues of servants.

Her change of residence accomplished, Mrs Grantham's next decision had been to replace the fast car preferred by her husband with a smaller Spanish-registered vehicle which would relieve her of the various complications, legal and practical, of continuing to drive the Lancia.

'Robert loved driving. I don't. In future, whenever I want to leave Spain, I shall fly,' she told Sarah, as the western suburbs of the city of Málaga merged with the outskirts of Torremolinos.

Soon the busy coast road, with two lanes going east and two west, brought them to Marbella, once a peaceful fishing village but now the most glitzy of all the resorts on the Costa del Sol.

'I see there's a Benetton shop here,' said Sarah, catching sight of the familiar name as they drove through the centre of the town.

'Is there? I hadn't noticed. I never come here except when I'm meeting or returning people to the airport,' her grandmother answered. 'Marbella's not my sort of place. It's for people with money to burn; pop stars, Arab sheikhs and, so one hears, lots of rich

crooks living on ill-gotten gains. But if you want to
go shopping, darling, you'll probably do much better
here than in Algeciras where I buy most of my things.'

'Apart from a pair of espadrilles, there's nothing
much I——' Sarah's reply tailed off as, among the
people strolling and window-shopping, she caught
sight of the Spaniard and the girl.

As before, at the airport, she was talking and he
was listening. The look on his face was one of amused
indulgence; an expression suggesting to Sarah that
although he was not greatly interested in what the girl
had to say, her sparkling dark eyes and the graceful
hand movements with which she was illustrating her
chatter gave him pleasure.

Noticing some people turning to stare at the
handsome couple, Sarah wondered if Carlos and his
companion might be dancers at one of Marbella's
fashionable night-clubs. It was easy to visualise them
dressed in the traditional costumes; the girl in a figure-
hugging dress which burst into a cascade of flounces
at the knee, the man in the tight black trousers and
bolero jacket of the male flamenco dancer.

Yet somehow she couldn't imagine him dancing for
his living. The girl, yes. In spite of her beauty, she
didn't look very intelligent. He did. No one with that
broad high forehead could be a simple soul, content
to spend every evening drumming his heels and
posturing for an audience of lobster-faced tourists. He
might have started as a dancer, but if he were still in
show business it would be as an impresario, she
thought.

'Someone you recognise?' asked her grandmother,
as Sarah looked over her shoulder to watch the
Spaniards out of sight. 'A lot of celebrities have villas
here, so I'm told. As I never go to the cinema and

don't see television, I shouldn't recognise the current crop if I saw them.'

'No, it wasn't anyone famous . . . just a girl who was on the plane with me and the man who met her at the airport,' Sarah answered.

Mrs Grantham surprised her by saying, 'Yes, I noticed them. Both very good-looking, but she won't keep her looks and he will.' She took her eyes off the road for a moment to meet her granddaughter's startled glance with a grin. 'Even at my advanced age, one still notices an attractive man, and he was extremely dishy . . . or whatever the latest expression for sex-appeal is!'

Leaving the shopping centre behind them, they came to the part of Marbella where, on the seaward side, the coast road was lined by luxurious hotels . . . the Meliá Don Pepe, the Marbella Club, the Puente Romano. Only the very richest visitors could afford to stay at such places, and although her grandmother spoke dismissively of them, Sarah felt some curiosity about what went on behind the high, well-watered hedges which screened the grounds from public view.

On the inland side of the road were the *urbanizaciones,* clusters of expensive villas, their verandahs wreathed with long bracts of crimson and purple bougainvillaea, their gardens shaded by date palms.

Further on they passed Puerto Banús, a village and marina which hadn't existed when her grandparents first came to Spain. Now, Sarah knew, its quays were lined with millionaires' yachts and, at night, the waterfront cafés were where the 'glitterati' went to see and be seen.

'What makes you think that Spanish girl will lose her looks but he won't?' she asked casually.

'Years of observation,' replied Mrs Grantham. 'Girls with her type of looks are exquisite when they're

young, but they tend to put on weight later and their
features coarsen rather than refine with age. The man
wasn't typically Spanish. Generally speaking the
present generation are inches taller than their parents
and grandparents because their lives aren't as hard
and they have a much better diet. But a man well over
six feet is still unusual in Spain, and he had excellent
bones. A very paintable face, I thought, didn't you?'

Painting was Molly Grantham's hobby and could
have been her profession if she had concentrated on
it. But as well as painting delightful watercolours of
the white villages in the hinterland of Andalusia, she
was also a talented cook and needlewoman who had
chosen to excel at being a wife, mother and hostess
rather than to make a career outside the home.

Sarah lacked artistic ability but shared her grandmother's other interests. For a long time during her
teens she had set her sights on becoming a veterinary
surgeon but, disappointingly, had failed to achieve the
necessary science results. It had been Molly Grantham
who had suggested caring for children as an alternative to attending to sick animals.

Sarah had had no difficulty in obtaining her certifi-
cate from the Nursery Nurse Examination Board. Her
first post had been with a couple with a new baby and
a toddler. When the baby was less than a year old,
the father, in public relations with an international
company, had accepted a posting to Canada. They
had wanted her to go with them, but at that time
Sarah had thought herself in love with Jamie Drayton.
Although sorry to miss seeing Canada, she had
preferred to stay near the boy she had loved since she
was fourteen to his seventeen.

At the time he hadn't been romantically interested
in her. That had come about later. Now she was
twenty-three and Jamie was pressing her to marry

him. The trouble was that she wasn't sure any longer that marriage to Jamie was still her heart's desire.

This was another reason for her visit to Spain. She needed a breathing space, far away from the pressure put on her by Jamie and by Harriet, her stepmother. Probably, while she was here, she would ask her grandmother's advice. For although the final decision was one only she could make, she felt that Molly Grantham's counsel, based on fifty years of happy marriage, would be much sounder than Harriet's.

Evidently Mrs Grantham had also been thinking about her former son-in-law's second wife. 'Harriet seems to have made a very good recovery from her operation,' she said. 'But it must have been a great relief to her to have you to take over the reins while she was in hospital and convalescing. What are you planning to do next, or haven't you decided?'

'Not really. There are several possibilities.' Sarah had caught sight of the sea and the bright yellow sail of a surfboard skimming across its glittering surface.

When wind-surfing was a new sport, her grandfather had bought a board for the use of the many people who stayed at his Spanish farmhouse and took picnics to the coast. Then, although in his sixties, he had taken up the sport himself. Remembering his wiry figure, at a distance distinguishable from his grandsons only by wind-blown white hair, she felt a sharp pang of sadness that he was no longer here to tease her and hug her and call her 'my pet' and 'sweetie'. She had loved him far more than her father.

Perhaps, years ago as a young man, before the death of his first wife, Colonel Lancaster had been more lovable. Perhaps it was Harriet's influence which gradually had changed him from the subaltern Sarah's mother had fallen in love with to the rather dour man he was now. Not that Harriet Lancaster was in any way the wicked stepmother of fairy tales. She had never been other than kind, in her brisk undemonstrative way, to her husband's three children and would have liked very much to add to the family.

Unfortunately that had proved impossible, and her inability to conceive a child of her own had culminated in the recent hysterectomy to which Mrs Grantham had referred.

Until the beginning of the Easter holidays Sarah had been working as assistant matron at a large preparatory school. After three terms in the job she had decided that, although it had been an interesting and often very amusing experience, she really preferred looking after pre-school children in a private household. As she had already given notice when Harriet announced her forthcoming operation, Sarah had felt an obligation to offer her services at home for as long as was necessary before looking for a new post.

Now, her duty to her stepmother satisfactorily discharged, she had the reward of a relaxed holiday with darling undemanding Granny who, unlike Harriet, wasn't obsessively house-proud and never gave advice unless asked for it.

At the same moment her grandmother was thinking that Sarah looked thoroughly pulled down by her stint as housekeeper-cum-nurse to that tedious woman Philip Lancaster had chosen as his second wife. Sarah had always been the Granthams' favourite among their grandchildren. From earliest childhood she had demonstrated the qualities of 'loving and giving' associated with the day of her birth; and although she wasn't eye-catchingly pretty like the Spanish girl at the airport, when she smiled she was truly beautiful. The trouble was that the lovely bubbly sense of fun which was the essence of her personality had for long been, if not extinguished, very much damped down by her father's and stepmother's lack of humour and gaiety. But after a day or two here she would blossom out, as she always did when she came to Spain, thought Mrs Grantham.

Aloud, she said, 'You'll find the flat rather small compared with Las Golondrinas.'

Her previous home had been named after the martins which every year built their mud nests on the rafters of the verandah. 'But I must say I like it much better than I expected to. It's very convenient to have the use of a large pool without the bother of maintaining it, and the gardens are all looked after by a nice man called Tomás, so I have more time for painting. Which reminds me, on Friday night there's a private view at the hotel. You don't have to come with me unless you feel like it, but it may be amusing.'

'I'd like to come,' said Sarah, admiring the fortitude with which her grandmother had adapted to her changed circumstances.

At the time of Grandpa's death, Sarah's instinctive reaction had been to drop everything and fly at once to Spain. However, as her uncle, the Granthams' eldest son, had pointed out after breaking the news to her, for everyone who loved Granny to descend on Las Golondrinas would be a burden rather than a help. Sarah had written a long loving letter of sympathy and from then on had made a point of writing more regularly than before, hoping the frequent letters would be a small comfort.

It wasn't until they had passed through the town of Estepona that the resort development began to thin out and it was possible to see what the Sun Coast had been like before hordes of northerners descended on it.

'The wild flowers are marvellous this year. I come back from my walks with great armfuls of them, and they last surprisingly well,' said Mrs Grantham.

A few moments later she was overtaken at high speed by the silver Porsche, also heading in the direction of the distant Rock of Gibraltar.

The fast car streaked past like a rocket, its metallic coachwork catching and reflecting the sunlight as it swept down a straight stretch of road and was soon lost to view round a bend.

'If there are a couple of *motoristas* lurking up ahead, that Brit will find himself paying out an instant fine,' remarked Molly Grantham, referring to the white-helmeted motorbike police who always rode about in pairs, empowered to impose instant penalties for traffic offences.

'It isn't a Brit,' Sarah told her. 'It's that Spaniard you noticed at the airport and I saw again in Marbella. Didn't you see his car when it passed us in the airport car park?'

'No, I didn't,' said her grandmother. 'I wonder why he's driving a car with a British number plate. Perhaps it belongs to someone else and he's borrowed it; although usually the owners of cars in that class aren't keen to let other people drive them. It was a Porsche, wasn't it?'

'Yes.'

'I thought so. It was a turbo Porsche your grandfather would have liked to own, had he been richer and younger. But they cost over thirty-five thousand, so it had to remain a pipe-dream. There weren't many things Robert wanted which he couldn't have, I'm glad to say.'

The tone of her voice echoed the spirit of her replies to Sarah's letters, in one of which she had written that almost fifty years of happy partnership was such extreme good fortune that gratitude rather than grief was her uppermost feeling.

A long-lasting love match like her grandparents' marriage had for long been Sarah's main ambition. A year ago, a wedding-ring chosen with Jamie had been at the top of the list of her personal pipe-dreams. Yet now that Jamie had finally discovered he loved her, she was no longer certain that being a country GP's wife was the future she wanted.

As they drove round a series of bends, each one giving an enticing glimpse of a sandy inlet lapped by pellucid water, Sarah found it was the man in the Porsche rather than the recently qualified Doctor James Drayton who occupied her thoughts.

She had thought she had seen the last of the Spaniard at Marbella. Now it appeared that his destination might also be Sotogrande. She might see him again. She wanted to see him again; not for the usual reason that a woman looked forward to another encounter with a man. Quite the reverse. It was merely that the way he had looked through her still rankled. She hoped for an opportunity to give him a taste of the same damping indifference.

On the afternoon of the private view party, Sarah swam thirty laps of the large swimming pool in the grounds of the low-built hotel which shared its entrance drive with the two-storey blocks of flats where her grandmother lived.

After her swim, she climbed out, rinsed off the chemicals in the water under the poolside shower and discreetly changed into a dry bikini before stretching out on a sun-bed to toast herself for the precise amount of time which would produce a tan without redness or peeling.

In spite of being fair, she tanned quickly and already was a better colour than on the day of her arrival.

She felt better, too; invigorated by the heavenly sun and long walks along flower-lined roads crossing the wide open spaces of moorland lying inland. All the strain of keeping house for her father and Harriet, cooking meals to suit their taste but not hers, had dissipated in a few days of her grandmother's much more delicious cuisine and undemanding companionship.

Sarah hadn't confided her dilemma to Mrs Grantham yet. There had been several opportunities, but she had chosen to keep it to herself for the time being. In bed at night and during her daily sunbathes, she tried to sort out her thoughts and emotions. But at night she usually fell asleep within minutes of climbing into bed, and when she was basking by the pool her mind tended to drift away from the questions she should be dwelling on to ponder comparative trivialities such as what to wear to the party tonight.

Not that it would be a proper party; just a roomful of people—'mostly old fogeys like me', her grandmother had warned her—going through the motions of being interested in the paintings on show when what had brought most of them there was the free wine and *tapas* and the gossip.

Still, at any gathering of people there was always a chance of making an interesting contact or even a new friend, Sarah thought drowsily, revelling in the golden warmth radiating on her almost bare body.

Unbidden, into her mind came the thought that *he* might be there, the Spaniard called Carlos. It was irksome to find herself still thinking about him and experiencing disappointment because she hadn't seen the silver car again. Every time she passed the hotel forecourt on her way to and from the pool she half expected to see it there. In Algeciras this morning she had looked for its distinctive aerodynamic design wherever there were cars parked.

Not that the somewhat down-at-heel port of Algeciras seemed likely to attract visitors from the de luxe Sotogrande estate which must be where he was staying, if indeed he were still in this area.

Her grandmother had driven her round the estate, which had a uniformed guard on duty in the security booth at the entrance, the day after her arrival. Like the best hotels at Marbella, most of the largest houses were secreted behind dense hedges or high white-washed walls topped with red Roman tiles. The shuttered upper windows of villas used for only a few weeks a year, the ubiquitous shimmer of sprinklers supplied from the estate's own bore-holes so that when water ran short in the surrounding areas, the gardens, polo grounds, golf courses and even the verges at Sotogrande were always kept moist and verdant, had given her an impression of the extravagant lifestyle of the people who owned property there.

It was a lifestyle which in some ways intrigued her and in others repelled her. The same could be said of her feelings about the driver of the silver Porsche, whose darkly bronzed dynamic features kept flashing on her mental screen as annoyingly as an advertise-ment interrupting a programme on commercial TV.

In the short time she had seen him at the airport and again in the car park, he had succeeded in exerting a strange and annoying fascination. At the same time he had repelled her simply by being too much. Any man with that face, that body, that car and heaven knows what else, had to have an outsize ego. So why couldn't she stop thinking about him?

Sarah sipped a glass of white wine and studied a painting of a herd of young bulls being driven through

a grove of cork oaks, their black hides contrasting
with the burnt orange trunks of the recently de-barked
trees, some of which she had seen in the countryside
near the hotel.

Golf rather than art seemed to be the most popular
topic at the private view, judging by snatches of
conversation distinguishable from the general buzz of
talk in the hotel's exhibition room.

On arrival she and her grandmother had been
received by the artist whose work was on show. She
was an American who had rented one of the flats for
an extended painting holiday. Several pictures had red
stickers on them, but Sarah suspected this might be a
device to encourage people to buy the others. She and
Mrs Grantham had been among the first-comers and
so far she hadn't seen anyone producing a wallet or a
cheque-book.

'And who might you be, young lady?' an elderly
man with a pale pink bow tie enquired.

Smiling, she introduced herself, learning that he and
his wife were migrants from Canada who also had a
winter place in Florida. There were very few local
people present. Nearly everyone, it seemed, was a
refugee from a colder region.

However, just as she was beginning to tire of making
small-talk to strangers in an increasingly smoky
atmosphere, a new group of people arrived. They were
led by a formidably elegant Spanish matron with
immaculately coiffed black hair, accompanied by
several young people, including the girl who had been
on the flight from London.

At the sight of her, Sarah tensed. If the girl was
here, it seemed a reasonable assumption that *he* was
somewhere about. She looked expectantly at the
doorway where, a few moments later, two men came
into view; one short and grey-haired and the

other . . . Her throat tightened with unwilling
excitement at the sight of the tall figure lingering on
the threshold of the room, surveying the assembly of
foreigners with a faintly sardonic expression as if he
hadn't much time for these invaders of his land whose
presence had brought prosperity but also much that
was vulgar and tawdry.

The older man was wearing a lounge suit and tie,
and bowing over women's hands. Carlos was more
informal in a light-coloured silk tweed sports coat
over an ivory shirt with the collar unfastened. His
manners too were less formal than those of the man
he had arrived with. (Not quite old enough to be his
father, thought Sarah.) On being greeted by a woman
who knew him, he shook hands without bowing or
bestowing a token kiss on the back of her palm.

Becoming aware that she was staring, she forced
herself to look away. Just then her grandmother
appeared at her elbow, saying, 'Are you getting bored,
dear? Shall we slip away?'

'I'm in no hurry to leave unless you want to go,'
Sarah answered. She noticed that Mrs Grantham's
glass was empty. 'Shall I get you another *vino*?'

By the time she got back from the drinks table,
Molly Grantham was talking to Erik and Kristen, a
Scandinavian couple. After some general conversation, he and Sarah's grandmother went to look at a
picture he was debating buying and Kristen began to
talk about riding, her favourite pastime.

'Are you going to watch the polo on Sunday
morning?' she asked.

'My grandmother hasn't suggested it; but as I've
never seen polo except on TV, it would be interesting
to watch it live,' Sarah answered.

'August's the best month,' said Kristen. 'That's
when the important matches are played. But there is

one top player staying at Sotogrande at the moment. He's here tonight. I saw him arriving not long ago.' She glanced round the room, caught someone's eye and waved. 'He's coming over,' she said, with a pleased expression. 'He's a ten-goaler. That's as good as they get.

Here it came, thought Sarah—the chance she had wanted to make it clear that the Spaniard wasn't God's gift to *every* girl. But if she were truly indifferent to him, she wouldn't be wondering if her lipstick needed freshening, she acknowledged, with rueful self-mockery.

'Hello, Carlos. How are you?' Kristen gave him her hand and this time he did perform the traditional obeisance.

'I'm fine, and you look terrific.' His English was perfect, without any trace of an accent.

Sarah wondered if Kristen would have responded to the compliment with such a flirtatious smile had her husband still been with them. It was a moment or two before she remembered to introduce Carlos to the English girl standing next to her. When she did perform the introduction, Sarah had the distinct impression that Kristen would like her to say hello and then drift tactfully away.

But in fact what happened was that after Kristen had begun, 'Sarah, this is Carlos Hastings . . . ' she was prevented from completing the introduction by the sudden appearance of someone else she knew who, with a perfunctory apology to the others, swept her away from them.

Thus it was the Spaniard and Sarah who were left standing together; she feeling oddly isolated with him in spite of all the people surrounding them.

'Hastings? As in the Battle of?' she enquired, with raised eyebrows. If it hadn't been for his flawless

English she would have thought she had misheard.

'That's right. I'm a hybrid,' he told her. 'Half English . . . half Spanish. How do you do? Or in my mother's language, *Encantado, señorita*.' His dark eyes, uninterested at the airport, now surveyed her more appreciatively, taking in the freshly washed, finger-combed tangle of curls, the after-six make-up, the frivolous ear-rings.

Clearly, this time she was making a stronger impression, aided no doubt by the fact that, apart from Kristen and the Spanish girl, she was the only young woman in sight.

Striving for coolness, not easy with Carlos Hastings looming over her, forced by shortage of space to stand as close as if they were dancing an old-fashioned waltz, her response was, 'How interesting. Which of your parents' cultures has the strongest influence on you, Mr Hastings . . . or should I say Señor?'

'Neither. You must call me Carlos. Even the Old Guard'—with a glance at the elderly people surrounding them—'get on to a first-name basis within minutes of meeting each other. To get back to your question, it's a difficult one for me to answer. I feel equally at home in both countries. However, my Spanish cousins, who are here with me tonight, tell me I'm nine-tenths English, and my English relations say the opposite.' A glint came into his eyes. 'You must judge for yourself . . . when we know each other better.'

The remark confirmed what instinct had already told her; in the games played by men and women, she was not in his league. A ten-goaler on the polo field, he was also an experienced philanderer who would quickly detect her own lack of experience in that sphere.

She had had the usual youthful dates, but her

unrequited love for Jamie had kept her from becoming seriously involved with anyone else. And Jamie himself, although as a medical student he had doubtlessly had one or two unserious relationships with pretty nurses, was not a man of vast experience like this Anglo-Spaniard. Jamie didn't approve of promiscuity. His profession had given him first-hand knowledge of the unhappy results of too much permissiveness. After telling Sarah he loved her, he had admitted he wouldn't have like it if she had lived with other men as had many of her contemporaries. At the time she had been overjoyed that he valued her for being a one-man girl. Later, some of his views about women had seemed rather priggish, and she hadn't been able to agree with all of his attitudes.

Trying not to blush under Carlos Hastings' close study of her face, she gave a slight shrug and answered, 'I'm not here for very long.'

She intended to give the impression that she wasn't particularly interested in getting to know him better. But either he didn't believe her or he took it as a cue to say, 'In that case we shouldn't waste time. You're not smoking, I notice.'

Slightly baffled by this apparent *non sequitur*, she said, 'No . . . I don't smoke.'

'Neither do I, and I find the fug in here unpleasant. There's a rather nice restaurant at the Cortijo Los Canos just up the road. We shan't have trouble getting a table at this time of year. Shall we cut and run?'

Deep down, she felt an impulse to answer, 'Yes, let's.' There was a side of her nature which would have liked nothing better than to agree to his suggestion. But it was the innermost part of her which, like the core of a pearl, had from childhood been overlaid with layers of imposed ideas about what was right and wrong, done or not done, wise or foolish. The

rebel in Sarah very rarely outvoted the steady responsible aspects of her character. If it had she wouldn't
have been so well suited to take care of other people's
children.

Only very occasionally, as now, did she feel a brief
surge of recklessness, a desire to do something which
her sensible self said was not on.

Firmly suppressing the impulse, she said, in her
primmest tone, 'Wouldn't your relations think that
rather rude? I feel sure my grandmother would. I'm
having dinner with her, here at the hotel.'

He would hardly have the effrontery to suggest that
he joined them, she thought. Or would he? She had
an uneasy feeling that this suave and worldly man
would not be easily put off once he set his sights on
something or someone. Perhaps she should be flattered
that tonight he found her worthy of his connoisseur's
attention. Although, as she had thought at the outset,
probably it was only because there was no one more
glamorous around.

'My relations don't expect me to spend all my time
with them,' he told her. 'I'm not their house guest. I
have a place of my own here. Which is your grandmother?' His height gave him a better view of the
crush of people than Sarah had. He added, 'Is she
wearing a blue dress to match her eyes?'

'Yes, but how did you guess?' she asked, surprised
by his perspicacity. 'Did you meet her before you met
me?'

'No, but I can see the likeness. Obviously she was
also a very striking girl when she was your age,' he
added gallantly.

It was on the tip of her tongue to retort, 'If you
really mean that, it's surprising you don't remember
seeing me before at the airport.' But she decided not

to give him the satisfaction of knowing she remembered him.

'Come and introduce me,' he said. Taking her by
the hand, he began to thread his way through the
crowd, drawing her along behind him as he asked
people to let him through.

As they had not shaken hands when Kristen had
started to introduce them, it was the first time he had
touched her. Sarah was sharply aware of the feel of
his long strong fingers enclosing hers in a way which
seemed rather intimate on so brief an acquaintance.

When he reached Mrs Grantham's side, he waited
for a pause in her conversation with a man with a
goatee beard before giving her a charming smile and
saying, 'Your granddaughter is going to introduce
me.' He glanced expectantly at Sarah.

'This is Carlos Hastings, Granny.'

'Ah, the driver of the silver Porsche. I'm Molly
Grantham. How do you do?'

He took her hand and bent over it. *'A sus pies,
señora.'*

'How nice to hear that expression again,' she said,
beaming at him. 'When my husband and I came to
live in Spain, years ago, I was enchanted to find that
a married woman was invariably greeted with "At
your feet, madam". But one hears it less often
nowadays. The old courtly manners seem to be dying
out—but not entirely, I'm glad to find.'

Trust him to know exactly how to win the good
opinion of someone of Granny's generation, thought
Sarah. For that matter, what woman of any age would
fail to be charmed by *A sus pies* uttered in textbook
Castilian, not the consonant-swallowing, difficult to
follow Andaluz dialect of the country people
hereabouts?

'How did you know I had a Porsche, Mrs Grantham?' he enquired.

'You passed us in it on your way back from the airport the day I went to meet my granddaughter,' she explained. 'You were meeting a very pretty girl. Your fiancée, perhaps?'

The man with the beard had tactfully drifted away by this time, leaving the three of them together.

Carlos smiled and shook his head. 'Isabel is lovely . . . but only nineteen. I am thirty-six, Mrs Grantham. She belongs to the Spanish side of my family. My father was English. Isabel and I are distant cousins. I went to meet her to save her parents the journey.'

'I see. That explains your car's British registration. We were puzzled by it, weren't we, Sarah? You spend more of your time in England than here, I gather?'

'Unfortunately, yes. Like most of the people in this room I prefer the climate of my mother's country. But the war—I mean the war here—brought hard times to her family. Even by the early fifties, when she was of marriageable age, my grandparents felt she would have a more comfortable life with the Englishman who admired her than with any of her Spanish suitors.' He glanced at Sarah. 'If you're a feminist that will shock you. But in fact the marriage arranged for her turned out very happily.'

Before she could deny that she was a feminist—or at least not one with extreme views—he turned back to her grandmother. 'I understand you and Sarah have arranged to dine here later. I wonder if I can persuade you both to be my guests at Cortijo Los Canos? Have you eaten there, Mrs Grantham? If not, I'm sure you'd enjoy the experience. The complex which includes the restaurant is an excellent example of how to put an old building to modern use without spoiling it.'

A few seconds elapsed before Mrs Grantham replied, 'I agree, it's a charming place. I've been to the buffet lunches they serve on Sundays, but I've never dined there. However as I've already booked a table here, why don't you join us tonight? Unlike your mother's compatriots, I'm not a night-owl, Mr Hastings. If you dine here with us, afterwards I can stroll back to my flat which is only a step away, leaving you and Sarah to stay up as long as you like.'

'That's a very thoughtful suggestion, but I should prefer you to dine with me. I have some old-fashioned ideas to go with my old-fashioned manners,' he told her, with a twinkle in his eyes. 'It would offend my Spanish sensibilities to be your guest at this stage. Perhaps we can compromise. Have dinner with me at Los Canos and then we'll return here for coffee and *digestivos*. That way you can go to bed early if you wish, or stay up with us if you feel like a late night for once. I should like to know what brought you to Spain and what you think of the country,' he added seriously.

If he was insincere in expressing a desire for her company as well as Sarah's, it was most convincingly done. His manner conveyed that Molly Grantham looked such an interesting woman that he hadn't noticed her age and would think it irrelevant anyway.

Inevitably, she allowed herself to be persuaded. But that she wasn't entirely bowled over by his charm was manifest a little later when, with her permission, he had gone off to cancel her booking and advise the other restaurant of their arrival.

'If that young man isn't a diplomat, he's missed his vocation,' she said dryly.

'I was told by Kristen that he's a ten-goal polo

player. Whether he does anything else, or is just a playboy, I don't know,' said Sarah.

Nor did she know whether to be glad or sorry that within fifteen minutes of their meeting Carlos had fixed a dinner date. At least with her grandmother acting as a duenna, things couldn't get out of hand.

Kristen reappeared. 'We are leaving now. I wondered if you would care to join me for a ride tomorrow morning, Sarah? There's a livery stable near here. I don't have my own horse. I hire one. That is, of course, if your grandmother doesn't mind my stealing you for an hour or two?' she added politely.

'Not in the least,' said Mrs Grantham. 'I'm sure Sarah would enjoy it very much. She used to be mad about horses in her early teens, but I think it's some time since you've done any riding, isn't it, darling?'

'Ages,' Sarah agreed. 'I should think an hour on horseback would be about my limit after so long out of the saddle. I don't want to cripple myself.'

Kristen arranged to call for her at the flat, bringing a spare pair of stretch-denim breeches.

'I think she is lonely for companions of her own age,' said Mrs Grantham, when the other girl had gone to join her husband. 'I assume she is Erik's second wife and young enough to be his daughter. They appear to be happy together and, like all Scandinavians, she adores this climate. But I suspect she's bored a good deal of the time. It's essential to have a lot of portable hobbies to be a happy expatriate. The social whirl has no real sustenance.'

Sarah said, 'When we were chatting earlier, she mentioned that she spoke several languages, including fluent *castellano*. Surely that must help? If most of the foreigners are old, can't she make friends with local people?'

'I doubt it. Although in general the Spanish are

very affable, they tend not to mix with outsiders socially. Nor do the French . . . or the English, for that matter. If you think about it, most friendships develop out of mutual interests, whether professional or personal. Kristen has nothing in common with her Spanish contemporaries who are either working or immersed in their children. As Robert and I found out long ago, there are differences in outlook which are very difficult to bridge. You won't notice it with Carlos Hastings because he is a mixture of two cultures. Even so, I don't think he was joking entirely when he mentioned his Spanish sensibilities. Men here are far, far more *macho* than Englishmen. The younger ones will push a pram and are very sweet with their children, but——'

By this time they had made their way out of the babel and smoke of the exhibition and were in the comparative peace of the hotel's spacious entrance lounge.

The sight of Carlos striding towards them made Mrs Grantham cut short her exposition on the Spanish male.

Very soon Sarah was tucked in the back of the Porsche with her grandmother in the front, being helped with the safety belt by Carlos.

She knew from previous visits to her grandparents that Spanish men, when dressed up to go out, usually trailed a strong, sometimes overpowering, odour of *colonia*. The only emanation from Carlos was the faintest whiff of some subtle after-shave which, without leaning forward to sniff, she couldn't be sure was Dior's *Eau Sauvage*.

Sitting behind her grandmother gave her a view of the way his thick glossy black hair would flick into curls on his collar if he grew it half an inch longer. Her eyes lingered on the slanting lines of his cheekbone and jaw, reminding her of Mrs Grantham's comment that he had excellent bones and would keep his looks late in life.

Apart from the luxurious car which he might have chosen for its performance rather than its opulent appearance, he was not a man for conspicuous extravagance, she noticed. He didn't wear rings and his watch, though it was expensive, was of unobtrusive design. These were points in his favour which might yet mount up and outweigh the things which made her wary of him.

Throughout the short drive to the restaurant, she was conscious of conflicting reactions to him; attraction but also antagonism. It would have been easier to handle this uncomfortable state of mind if it hadn't been complicated by a third element—her unresolved dilemma over Jamie.

The Cortijo Los Canos was a peach-coloured building with a central courtyard entered through a high arched passage. In the middle of the courtyard was the top of a well, its low wall surrounded by many pots of geraniums, their bright petals blanched by the moonlight.

From the courtyard two outdoor staircases gave access to a first floor door and a gallery with rooms behind it. These and the rooms below were being used as business premises which at this time of night were closed because, even in Spain with its idiosyncratic opening hours, the working day was at an end and, long after the rest of Europe, the Spanish were starting to think about dining.

Looking up at a balcony with more geraniums spilling between its black rails, Sarah said, 'I know *cortijo* means farm. What does *los canos* mean?'

Mrs Grantham said, 'I looked it up the first time I came here. *Cano* has several meanings, ranging from white-haired to venerable. I concluded the place had originally been a small monastery and the brothers were known as *los canos* by the villagers. Was I right?'

Carlos shook his head. 'An intelligent deduction, but in fact it's the name of the family who used to own the property.'

In the restaurant, the head waiter bowed and said in English, 'Good evening, ladies . . . Don Carlos.' Evidently their host was well known to him.

'Shall we go straight to our table?' Carlos suggested. 'I'm sure Sarah must be hungry even if you have adapted to Spanish meal-times, Mrs Grantham.'

Their table was half way along the lofty dining-room, close to one of the windows overlooking the courtyard. *Copitas* of pale dry sherry were brought with the menu folders. Damask napkins were shaken out and spread on their laps. Small boat-shaped dishes of olives and thinly-cut slices of *chorizo* were presented for them to nibble.

When their decisions had been made and Carlos had chosen a white wine for the seafood starters and a red wine to drink with the lamb, Molly Grantham said, 'Apropos what you were telling us about your parents' marriage, I'm intrigued to know how an Englishman managed to impress your grandparents with his superior qualities. This happened in Madrid, presumably?'

'No, no . . . my mother's family lived here in the south. If you drive a few kilometres up the road which passes the golf course, there comes into view, in the distance, what looks like a ruined castle but is actually a fortified village.'

'We saw it this morning,' said Sarah. 'We took a roundabout route to Algeciras and passed through a modern village where, Granny was told, the people from the old village had been re-housed.'

'That's correct. Many villages in Spain have become uninhabited either because they're too remote or lack a good water supply to keep the land round them fertile. The background to my parents' marriage is linked to a story you're sure to hear if you ever go to Arcos de la Frontera midway between here and Sevilla.'

'I have been there. Sarah hasn't,' said her grand-mother. 'If I was told any stories about the town I'm afraid I've forgotten them. It was some time ago.'

Carlos offered her the olives. 'In 1917 when the Duke of Osuna found himself ruined financially, he auctioned his castle. It was bought, for a song, by an Englishwoman, Mrs Violeta Buck, who became so identified with Andalusia that she always dressed in white. Later the castle was inherited by her niece, Dakma Williams-Buck, who married the Marques de Tamarón. As a young man my father stayed with them and decided to see if any more castles were going at give-away prices. By the time he arrived in this area, he'd rather gone off the idea, but as he'd been given an introduction to my grandparents, he felt it would be rude not to call. The place was already falling apart. He wouldn't have had it as a gift. But he took one look at my mother and, for them both, it was *el flechazo*——love at first sight.'

'How romantic!' said Molly Grantham.

'Only because he happened to be the grandson of Maximilian Hastings,' he remarked drily. 'But for that advantage, he would have been politely sent packing and I shouldn't exist.'

Although she had little interest in high finance, Sarah had heard of Maximilian Hastings, founder of the merchant bank of that name. But as Hastings was not an uncommon surname, she hadn't immediately connected Carlos with the great banking family. No wonder he could afford to run a Porsche and play polo if he was a member of that affluent dynasty. They were as rich as the Rothschilds.

As the evening progressed they learned little more about him. He was at pains to draw them out, addressing himself mainly to Mrs Grantham although at frequent intervals his dark eyes rested on Sarah with a quizzical gleam, as if he knew she was puzzled by the motive behind his interest in them.

His behaviour in asking them out and concentrating his attention on her grandmother might have made sense if he himself had been struck by *el flechazo*, the literal meaning of which must be an arrow-shot. But that, clearly, was out of the question. If it had happened to his father, he must have been considerably younger than Carlos was now. Good-looking men of thirty-six didn't lose their hearts on sight, especially not to a girl who a few days before hadn't rated a second glance.

A more probable explanation was that, with anyone who seemed resistant, he had developed a technique of behaving with great circumspection at the beginning, lulling them into believing he only looked like a womaniser but was really quite safe and harmless.

Anyone who would believe that would believe anything, thought Sarah, noticing the way other women in the restaurant kept glancing in his direction.

Nevertheless, secure in her grandmother's presence, she relaxed and enjoyed herself. In most social situations, she tended to be a listener rather than a talker. Tonight, animated by the wine, she recounted a few of the funnier incidents during her time as an assistant school matron, and succeeded in making her grandmother wipe away tears of mirth while Carlos showed his white teeth as he shook with laughter.

'Just as well it was a preparatory school. Had it been a school for older boys, you would have been rushed off your feet with seniors reporting sick,' he remarked. 'Matrons were never young and attractive in my day. The Sister in charge of the sick bay at my boarding school was known as the Gorgon.'

The compliment, and the look which accompanied it, made Sarah's colour deepen even with Granny sitting between them.

She said, 'I dare say you needed someone like that to keep you in order. Some of my little boys were so homesick and miserable they wouldn't say bo to a goose. I can't believe you were ever a timid shrimp.'

He smiled at her. 'Probably not. Which was just as well, because I was packed off at eight. Which, as up to that point I'd been brought up on Spanish lines, was rather a traumatic change.'

'I feel eight is much too young for a child to be sent away from home,' said Molly Grantham. 'Was that at your father's insistence?'

'No, it was my uncle's idea. My father was a fanatically keen member of the St Moritz Toboggan Club . . . the club which organises the Cresta run. He used to spend most of the Cresta season at St Moritz. We'd go over there before Christmas and stay till the beginning of March. I used to have a few lessons with a retired schoolmaster, but spent most of my time on skis. One year I was left at our chalet while my parents visited friends. They were killed in a cable-car accident. The rest of my education was arranged by my father's eldest brother, whose own sons were ten years my senior and who thought I needed anglicising. I was therefore despatched as a boarder without delay. Apart from the food, I enjoyed it,' he concluded cheerfully. 'As Sarah has shrewdly surmised, I was never the shy, sensitive type.' He beckoned the waiter to enquire about puddings.

The discovery that he had experienced an even more shattering bereavement than her own loss of her mother, after a protracted illness, when Sarah was eleven, made her see him in a new light.

She knew how indulgent the Spanish were with their children. Only this morning, at the market, she had heard little girls being told how pretty they were, and little boys also being praised. It was rare to see a child smacked or scolded, yet they were no less well behaved than their English counterparts. To have been abruptly translated from the care of a fond Spanish mother to the communal life of a prep school must, whatever he said now, have been a shocking experience.

She was reminded of Yusef, the small overweight Arab princeling who, brought up among the women of his petrocrat father's household, had been sent to the school where she worked and had been, at first, deeply unhappy. Unless a careful watch was kept by the staff, foreign pupils could have a tough time at an English boarding school. The natural bullies and their followers were quick to spot any abnormality from sticking-out ears to alien personal habits. Twenty-seven years ago, at a school with poor supervision, an olive-skinned orphan could have found himself in purgatory.

They ate pears poached in wine and then drove back to the hotel to have coffee and liqueurs with small juicy strawberries encrusted in caramelised sugar.

After a second cup of coffee, Mrs Grantham said, 'Thank you so much for a delicious dinner, Carlos. Now please don't insist on escorting me to my front door, because there's not the least need. Old ladies can quite safely trot about here at night, I'm glad to say.'

'I disagree with that most inappropriate description of you, but I think you are right to feel safe here,' he said, as they rose. 'There are places in Spain where a woman is no longer safe on her own after dark, but this isn't one of them. Goodnight, Molly.' (She had asked him to use her first name.) 'I hope you'll invite me to see *your* paintings before I return to England.'

Sarah stood up. 'I think I should come with you, Granny. I want to be up early in the morning to do some limbering up exercises before riding with Kristen.'

She expected Carlos to protest that the night was still young and to pressure her to stay and talk to him. To her surprise, he didn't.

'If you're both deserting me, I shall certainly walk you home,' was all he said.

The flats were built on sloping ground which had been laid out so that each downstairs flat had its own piece of garden—those on the first floor had large balconies—as well as the shared stretches of garden surrounding the wide brick paths and steps which gave access to every block and connected them with each other.

One of the thin homeless cats which Tomás chased off if he saw them, but which had long since discovered that Mrs Grantham was a soft touch for left-overs, shot across the path ahead of them as they strolled back. The air was still warm and fragrant with night-scented flowers. From one of the occupied flats came the sound of a piano sonata.

Sarah wondered what would have happened if she had stayed with Carlos and they had walked back later. Would he have taken her hand again? Kissed her goodnight?

Her grandmother's flat and three others shared an entrance hall. Carlos opened the outer door for them and waited until Mrs Grantham had unlocked her front door and switched on the light in the lobby before he bade them goodnight. He didn't say anything to Sarah about seeing her again.

'I'm going to have a glass of water. What about you?' asked Mrs Grantham, turning into her tiny kitchen which was on the same side of the building as the entrance.

The window was open, screened by mosquito netting. They could hear his brisk footsteps retreating along the brick path. By the time Mrs Grantham had taken a bottle of Lanjaron water from the refrigerator and filled two tall glasses, the sound had died away.

Sarah found herself regretting giving that rather feeble reason for coming back now. He must have known it was an excuse to avoid being alone with him. Maybe the reason he hadn't pressed her to stay was that at some stage of the evening he had decided the quarry wasn't worth the chase.

The following morning, mounted on two good-natured hacks from the livery stable, Kristen and Sarah rode across the wild moorland bordering the four thousand four hundred acres of Sotogrande.

As the summer advanced, the sun would burn down on this landscape with a relentless heat which would make the brush dry and brittle, easily ignited. But in winter, according to Kristen, this corner of Andalusia received a good deal of rain, which was why at the moment it was a paradise of flowers.

Kristen *was* lonely. Mrs Grantham had been right about that. Already she had confided that she wished they lived nearer Marbella where there was more to do and more younger people.

'But Erik prefers it here,' she had said, with a shrug

and a sigh, as they rode through a cork wood, soon
after setting out.

Now it was time to turn back in the direction of
the sea which, from this height and distance, was a
sheet of pearl-coloured satin with no visible horizon.

'Do you have a boy-friend, Sarah?' Kristen enquired.

Sarah said, 'Not at the moment,' and left it at that.

She wished Kristen hadn't asked. On this glorious
golden morning, surrounded by drifts of giant pink
clover, columbine and wild lupins, with the breeze
smelling like a *bouquet garni* after blowing over miles
of rosemary, thyme and other herbs, she didn't want
to think of anything but the beauty of the landscape
and the pleasure of being on horseback again.

They were returning through the cork wood when
another rider came into view. Sarah looked at the
horse first. It was a large light grey stallion, a much
more spirited animal than the two sedate geldings she
and Kristen were riding.

Then she looked at the rider and, with a thrust of
excitement, recognised Carlos Hastings.

Seeing that there wasn't room for the three horses
to pass without someone giving way, and thinking the
mettlesome grey might not take kindly to being held
up, she checked her obedient chestnut and drew into
line behind Kristen.

'*Hola! Buenos dias,*'Carlos greeted them, smiling.

He was wearing white riding-breeches, which showed
off long powerful thighs, and a checked cotton shirt
with the sleeves rolled up to display sinewy forearms
only lightly covered with black hairs. A glimpse of a
burnished bronze chest was visible where the shirt was
open to the second button. His hair was still wet from
the shower.

Years before, when her every spare moment had
been spent at the local riding-stables, Sarah had been

told by an old groom that a stallion would give no trouble, even in the company of other horses, if he was ridden by a confident horseman.

It seemed that he had been right, for the grey gave no sign of annoyance at meeting the two geldings or at having to wait while the riders conversed.

'I'm late this morning,' said Carlos. 'A call from London delayed me, or I should have joined you.' The remark was addressed to them both.

'What a beautiful horse,' said Sarah, admiring the grey's crested neck, veiled by a long snowy mane.

As she spoke, the grey raised his head and gave what looked like a strongly affirmative nod. Sarah and Carlos both laughed.

'He agrees with you,' he said.

They didn't stay talking long. A few minutes later Carlos moved off in the direction from which they had come, and the girls continued towards the stables.

Before resuming her place alongside Kristen, Sarah couldn't resist glancing over her shoulder at the stallion and his tall rider.

Kristen saw her look back. 'That horse Carlos rides makes me nervous. I don't trust stallions.'

After a slight pause, she added, 'I shouldn't trust Carlos either, if I were you.'

CHAPTER TWO

'WHY do you say that?' asked Sarah.

Kristen gave her a smouldering look, but Sarah sensed that the other girl's anger was not directed at her but at the man riding inland.

'He's already done his best to get me to have an affair with him. Now I think his eye is on you,' the Scandinavian girl replied. 'I suppose he's decided I'm a waste of his time and hopes you will be more co-operative. His attitude towards women is the same as that of safari hunters years ago, before cameras replaced rifles. To Carlos women are like big game was to those hunters.'

'If he made a pass at you, I'm surprised you're still friendly with him,' said Sarah, remembering Kristen's reaction to his greeting the night before.

'If I weren't, Erik would guess the reason and it would upset him. Also it isn't wise for foreigners to make enemies among the Spanish. Carlos has influence around here. If I were unpleasant to him, he might decide to teach me a lesson. He didn't like being turned down. If I gave him the cold shoulder publicly, he might decide to revenge himself by having us deported. We are only guests in this country—we could be told to leave if a Spaniard made a complaint about us. It has happened, so I'm told.'

'I can't believe he would do that,' Sarah exclaimed.

'Perhaps not . . . but it's better to keep on the right side of him.' Kristen gave Sarah a sideways glance. She seemed to be hesitating on the brink of some further revelations. 'It wasn't so much the pass that upset me. A lot of men think that because I'm married to an older man I must be bored and looking for a younger lover. I *am* bored sometimes. Erik spends so much of his time watching birds—that kind of bird,' she added, pointing at a pair of colourful hoopoes skimming among the trees ahead. 'And he doesn't want children,' she went on. 'He already has three by his first wife, and that is enough for him. He doesn't want to be woken in the night by a crying baby.'

'Did you know that when you married him?' asked Sarah, puzzled by why someone as attractive as Kristen should have chosen a husband twenty years her senior.

'Yes, he told me, and it didn't seem important. Now I do regret it. I've begged him to change his mind, but he won't. It was after a quarrel about it that I first met Carlos. He saw that I was unhappy and he was sympathetic and kind. I realised later that he was never really interested in my problem. He thought it would make me an easier conquest. It almost did. If he had had a little more patience, I might have joined the list of women who have had affairs with him. But he made his play before the plum was quite ripe for plucking,' Kristen said, with a catch in her voice. The quick way she averted her face made it plain that what had happened still had the power to distress her.

A few moments later, once more in command of herself, she said, 'Of course it's different for you. You're single, you can have affairs. I expect an affair with Carlos could be a lot of fun—as long as you didn't take him seriously. Some of his girl-friends have made the mistake of falling for him. When that happens, he drops them like, as you say, a hot potato.'

Sarah found herself curiously depressed by Kristen's revelation that Carlos had tried to engage her in an illicit affair. It seemed unworthy of him—unworthy of the man he could have been had his character matched his appearance.

She wondered how much the loss of both parents at the tender age of eight, and thereafter being in the care of a stern-sounding uncle, had affected his development. Perhaps he would have been different if his mother had lived. Certainly it would have made a great difference to her own life if her mother had been there to steer her through adolescence with sympathy and humour. Harriet, who wore no make-up herself and wasn't interested in clothes, had been no help at all in that respect. Nor had she been supportive in Sarah's battles with what her stepmother had dismissed as puppy fat which would eventually disappear of its own accord.

In fact plumpness had still been a problem when Sarah was nineteen. She had only slimmed down to her present slenderness after six months of rigorous self-discipline. Looking back, she could see now that her teenage tubbiness had been a direct result of losing her mother and acquiring a stepmother with whom she had nothing in common. Food, horses and romantic daydreams about Jamie had all been substitutes for the close, loving relationship she had had with her mother, and lost.

Since then she had trained herself out of eating for comfort and, although this morning's ride had been extremely enjoyable, horses were no longer a big thing in her life. Which left Jamie. Did she still love him or didn't she? Everyone who knew them seemed to think they were right for each other. As she had herself, right up to the moment when Jamie had said, 'Shall we make it official? Shall we get engaged?'

Alongside her, on the next sun-bed, Mrs Grantham looked over the top of an American bestseller she had borrowed from the lending library at the golf club.

'That's a very un-carefree expression for someone on holiday,' she remarked.

Realising she had been frowning, Sarah mustered a smile. 'I was digging about in my memory, trying to remember who said something to the effect—Be careful what you wish for, you may get it. Can you remember?'

Putting down the book, Mrs Grantham removed her spectacles and also the wide-brimmed straw hat with which she shaded her eyes when reading in sunlight. Like her granddaughter she was wearing a bikini, although there was rather more of hers than the minimal triangles of lime-green cotton on Sarah's sleek sun-oiled body.

Raising her hand to signal the waiter who was looking down from the hotel terrace where they had lunched, she said, 'No, I don't know who said it but I think there's a good deal of truth in it.' After a pause, she added, 'Don't you?'

Before Sarah had replied, the waiter arrived.

'*Si, señora*?' He was young. His glance strayed to the sun-streaked hair and golden body on the next lounger.

When he had gone to fetch two iced Cokes, Sarah said, 'Granny, may I ask you something rather personal?'

'Of course, darling.'

'When you were young . . . after you'd met Grandpa . . . were you ever attracted to anyone else? Or did loving him make you immune to all other men?'

Her grandmother polished the lenses of her sun-glasses and pondered the question for some moments.

'It didn't make me incapable of seeing that other

men were attractive,' she said thoughtfully. 'But I can truthfully say I was never drawn to anyone else. I always felt that in Robert I'd found the right man for me . . . the only man really. Of course if we hadn't met, we should both have found other people with whom to be happy, I expect. Common sense tells one that. And yet, looking back, I can't think of anyone I knew whom I might have loved if Robert hadn't materialised.' She put on the glasses and turned her face up to the sun. 'Those who were attractive weren't always likeable. And those who were nice weren't necessarily attractive. A husband needs to be both.'

'Did you and Grandpa ever have fights . . . times when you didn't get on?'

'Oh, yes, we had quite a few rows, especially at first,' Mrs Grantham admitted candidly. 'None of them ever very serious, and after a while we learned not to exasperate each other. But how could two strong-minded people live together for almost half a century without an occasional cross word? We never did see eye to eye on some things. But what I remember about our life, what I miss most, are the jokes. We had the same sense of humour and we spent a lot of time laughing.'

Her eyes on the still and shining surface of the pool, in which no one was swimming at the moment, Sarah was reminded of how she and Carlos had looked at each other and laughed when the stallion seemed to nod his head during their meeting in the cork wood that morning.

Was laughter a major component of her relationship with Jamie? They had shared some hilarious moments, they must have, even if she couldn't think of many offhand. But seriousness rather than wit was the keynote of his character. He didn't lack a sense of humour, but his eye for the funny side of things wasn't as sharp as her grandfather's had been or as she thought Carlos's might be.

She saw the waiter returning with two tall glasses on a tray.

'You must let me pay for these, Granny.' She reached for her beach-bag.

Presently, placing her glass on the grass in the shade of her sun-bed, her grandmother said, 'Dearest, I don't want to pry, but you've seemed a little distraite at times since your arrival. Is there something on your mind . . . or someone? Tell me to mind my own business if you don't want to discuss it.'

'I'd like to discuss it,' said Sarah, glad of the cue. 'I'm in such a muddle, Granny. You see, Jamie Drayton has asked me to marry him and, all at once, after thinking for ages that it was what I most wanted, I find I'm not sure any more. Not sure at all. Father and Harriet are furious with me. Well, perhaps not furious, but certainly not very pleased. They can't understand it. Nor can Dr and Mrs Drayton. They all thought it was a foregone conclusion.'

'How do they come to know about it if you and Jamie haven't settled the matter between yourselves yet?' asked her grandmother.

'He mentioned it to his mother and she decided to tell Harriet.'

'Not very sensible, considering that you and Harriet have never been close confidantes. So now you're under pressure from four other people as well as Jamie himself? I shouldn't allow that to weigh with you. If you have any doubts about your feelings, it's much wiser to wait. Are you afraid that, if you do, you might lose him and find yourself regretting it?'

Sarah shook her head. 'I don't think I have any rivals ready to seize him on the rebound. He'll wait for however long it takes me to make up my mind.

But my mind *was* made up . . . for years. It's only lately that I've begun to have doubts, and some of them aren't to do with Jamie so much as the life we would live . . . taking over his parents' house when Dr Drayton retires, which he wants to as soon as possible . . . settling down in the village where we were born and grew up. Somehow it seems so dull to spend almost the whole of one's life in the same place.'

'I think you made a mistake in not going to Canada when you had the opportunity,' said Mrs Grantham.

'I know I did,' Sarah agreed. 'I suppose recognising that error of judgment has undermined my confidence about making the right decision now.'

'You said some of your doubts aren't to do with Jamie . . . implying there are others which are. What are they?' her grandmother enquired.

Sarah swirled the Coke in her glass, making the ice cubes clink. 'It's hard to explain,' she said slowly. 'I—I'm still terribly fond of him. I can't bear the thought of hurting him. But there's no magic any more. I used to get more of a kick when he accidentally touched my hand in the days when I was a sort of kid sister to him than I do now when he kisses me. It's nice, but it isn't the bliss I imagined it would be. Perhaps I was expecting too much.'

'It would certainly be very foolish to agree to marry any man, however nice in other ways, if you have serious doubts about your physical rapport. On the other hand, it has to be said that love isn't always "a wonder and wild desire" from the outset,' said Mrs Grantham. 'I think it's rather like cookery. Some people have a natural gift for it, and others need a recipe book and a good deal of practice before they're successful. I wish I'd met Jamie Drayton. I knew you had a big crush on him when you were younger, but as you haven't said or written much about him for the last couple of years, I assumed it had died a natural death, as first love usually does.'

'I did think of asking you if I could bring him down with me,' Sarah told her. 'He wanted to come. He suggested it. But then I thought bringing him here would seem like a definite commitment and it would be better to come on my own and view the situation from a distance. Incidentally, he wasn't very happy about my taking the Lancia back to England for you. We had a bit of a clash about it. He thought I might get into trouble and not be able to cope. What could possibly go wrong on the motorail journey from Algeciras to Paris, I can't imagine. But he seemed to think something might and I shouldn't be able to handle it.'

She delved in her bag and from the back of her billfold produced a photograph of Jamie which she passed to her grandmother.

Following Colonel Lancaster's second marriage, his former in-laws had given up visiting him when they were in England. If Mrs Grantham had ever encountered Jamie during the time when his father was her daughter's GP she was unlikely to remember him.

'He certainly has a very pleasant face . . . intelligent . . . open . . . kind,' she said, after studying the picture for several minutes.

'Yes, he's all those things—and more,' Sarah agreed. 'He'll be a marvellous successor to his father because he has all the qualities which make old Dr Drayton so popular combined with up-to-date knowledge. I feel it's rather a shame for Jamie to bury himself in a country practice. He had it in him to do great things . . . become a consultant at one of the London teaching hospitals. But he doesn't like living in London, and also he knows his father wants him to take over from him, as he did from Jamie's grandfather in 1947 or whenever it was.'

'Would you have preferred Jamie to specialise? Would you have liked living in London?'

'Yes, I believe I should. But it's too late now. He's made his decision and I expect it's the best for him, if not for me. I really dislike the idea of going back to live in a place where everyone has known me since birth and where, if not breathing down my neck, Harriet will still be keeping an eye on me.'

At this point their conversation was brought to an end by the arrival of someone who knew her grandmother and came to chat to her before having a swim.

Later, when they had returned to the flat and were preparing a salad for their supper, Mrs Grantham said, 'By the way, while you were out riding this morning, I wrote a letter of thanks to Carlos Hastings. Later, when I went shopping, I took it round to the estate office to ask for his address. Who should come in while I was there but Carlos himself. They had a whole sheaf of very long Telex messages for him, which rather suggests that he's in close touch with London even when he's on holiday. He said he had also been riding and had seen you and Kristen.'

'Yes, I forget to tell you. We did see him—very briefly.'

For some reason Sarah refrained from telling her what Kristen had said about him.

'He wanted to know if we would be watching the polo and I said yes, we'd be there,' said Mrs Grantham.

'Oh . . . did you?' Sarah wished her grandmother hadn't committed them.

Carlos might get the wrong impression if he saw her among the spectators. He might think she was ready and willing to engage in a casual affair with him; that her behaviour last night had been merely playing hard to get.

After a early meal they went back to the hotel to watch one of the video films which were shown several times a week in the television room. A black comedy starring Jack Nicholson, it distracted Sarah from her problems for a couple of hours, and it was the film they discussed before going to bed.

But when she had opened the apricot glazed chintz curtains which had come from Las Golondrinas, and turned out the bedside lamp, as she lay looking at the stars her thoughts turned again to the man she had known all her life and the man she had met little more than twenty-four hours ago.

And it was the mocking dark face of the man who, when women fell in love with him, dropped them like hot potatoes, rather than the pleasant features of the one who wanted her to marry him, which dominated her mind's eye before she fell asleep.

It wasn't necessary to understand the intricacies of polo to find it an exciting game, Sarah discovered when she and Mrs Grantham stood on the sidelines watching eight horsemen wheeling their nimble ponies back and forth in pursuit of the ball.

With only four men in each team, they had no difficulty in distinguishing the players as the game veered this way and that between the goalposts.

As a team, the men in red shirts were the better players. But the men in white were captained by Carlos Hastings, whose unerring swings with his long-handled mallet combined with his brilliant horsemanship more than compensated for the deficiencies of the three other men on his side.

The game was very hard on the horses, which no

doubt was why each chukka lasted only seven minutes and thirty seconds. But Sarah noticed that Carlos rode his polo pony with much greater economy of effort than the other seven.

Mrs Grantham had parked her car well away from where the reserve ponies were tethered and the players cooled down between chukkas. Once or twice, while he was dismounted, Sarah thought she saw him glance in their direction; but while the game was in progress she could tell, even at a distance, that he was wholly intent on what he was doing.

At half time, all the regular spectators hurried to do what was apparently expected of them.

'It's called "stamping in the divots",' a horsey Englishwoman explained, urging Sarah and her grandmother to take part in tramping down the clods of earth displaced by the ponies' hooves, especially in front of the goalposts where the grass was badly cut up.

Only once did the play come within a few feet of where Sarah was standing. As four or five sweating ponies converged in a headlong gallop and thundered directly towards them, Mrs Grantham instinctively stepped back. Equally instinctively, Sarah moved protectively in front of her, although she had no real fear that they were about to be trampled.

Carlos was not in the thick of the mêlée at this point. He came streaking in from one side with a burst of speed which evoked an excited cheer from his team's supporters.

As the ball rolled towards the white line marking the edge of the field, followed by the tightly bunched ponies of the men in pursuit, he swept through the narrowing gap, his mallet scything the air and sending the ball to mid-field in a perfectly judged, strong, clean pass.

A cheer went up, followed by clapping. In a jostling bunch, the players swung in the opposite direction and, as swiftly as it had approached, the game moved away down the field.

Mrs Grantham sighed with relief and Sarah stopped holding her breath with an excitement which had as much to do with the momentary nearness of the tall white-clad rider as with the risk to their safety which he had skilfully averted.

'That was too close for comfort! I thought for a minute we were going to be mown down like mushrooms,' her grandmother remarked. 'Oh, look . . . he's scored again!'

Soon after this the game ended with the white-shirted team in the lead by twelve goals to seven.

'Shall we go?' Sarah suggested.

She sensed that her grandmother had been more shaken than she would admit. For her own part she had no wish to hang about now the game was over.

'Yes, but first we must just walk over and congratulate Carlos. Not to do so would be discourteous when he wined and dined us so well the night before last.'

'He'll be surrounded by cronies. Now that you have his address, wouldn't a note be better?' Sarah suggested.

Mrs Grantham looked at her keenly. 'Do you dislike Carlos, Sarah?'

'I have reservations about him.'

'How odd. I find him a charming man—and obviously attracted to you,' Mrs Grantham added.

'I should think he's attracted to anyone young and female who's not impossibly plain,' Sarah said drily.

'I see nothing wrong with that—in a bachelor,' said her grandmother. 'Although at his age, I suppose, he may have been married and is now divorced or separated.'

Somehow this was not a possibility which had occurred to Sarah before. She was surprised to find how much she disliked the idea that Carlos might have a broken marriage behind him. It was even more unacceptable than the image projected by Kristen of an unscrupulous womaniser.

'Anyway, he's too old for you . . . if you *had* liked him . . . and if you'd been free,' went on Mrs Grantham.

'I am free,' Sarah protested.

'Technically, yes. But until you've made up your mind about Jamie's proposal, you are bound to him to some degree, my dear. After all, now more than ever, a man doesn't ask a girl to marry him unless he expects her to say yes. I don't think you can count yourself free until you've either turned him down or accepted him,' said her grandmother.

A Range Rover came towards them and stopped alongside their car. The driver was Carlos. As he climbed out and walked round the bonnet, they saw he had taken off his helmet and also the stout leather pads which had protected his knees while he was in the saddle. His black hair was damp with sweat. His tanned face glistened. A hand towel was wrapped round his neck and tucked inside the unbuttoned neck opening of the thin cotton polo shirt which, like his hair, was damp and clinging to his torso.

'I hope you don't mind my joining you before I've showered and changed. I've brought some champagne,' he told them, before opening the nearside door and taking from the passenger's side a coolbox and two light-alloy folding chairs.

'I'm sorry you had nothing to sit on while you were watching, Mrs Grantham. These were in use during the game or I should have had them sent over to you earlier.'

'Sarah and I were just debating whether to come and congratulate you on walking away with the match, or whether to leave it until later to tell you how much we enjoyed that very exciting game,' said Molly Grantham, as he set up a chair for her.

'I'm glad you found it exciting.' He placed another chair for Sarah. 'Someone who was watching the play through field-glasses tells me there was one point at which it was probably more alarming for you than exciting. I hope you weren't too unnerved when the ball came close to you both. I assure you that, although we sometimes damage ourselves, we very rarely do any harm to the onlookers.'

'I'm sure you don't. It was foolish of me to be nervous, which I was—for a moment,' she admitted. 'Sarah is made of sterner stuff. It was very courageous of you to step in front of me, darling. You're your father's daughter.' She explained this remark to Carlos by adding, 'My son-in-law holds the Military Cross for gallantry.'

A bright flush of embarrassment flooding her cheeks, Sarah said, 'Father's action and mine are hardly comparable, Granny. I wasn't being brave. I'm more used to horses than you are.'

'You have nice light hands,' said Carlos. 'I noticed that the other morning. Some of the visitors who hire horses from the stables must give the poor brutes hell. I should hate to be a livery horse in my next incarnation.'

He had opened the coolbox and was removing the wire mesh from a bottle of champagne. French champagne, Sarah noticed, not the Spanish imitation, although, to her inexpert palate, there was nothing wrong with the best brands.

'I've already slaked my thirst with a litre of *agua mineral* ,' he said, easing the cork from the neck of the bottle.

A few moments later three glasses of pale golden wine were standing on the lid of the coolbox, bubbling and sparkling in the sun. He handed one to Mrs Grantham, the second to Sarah, and took up the third glass himself.

'Salud,' he said to her grandmother, touching his glass to hers and then, as she echoed the toast, taking a sip of champagne.

'Salud——' he repeated to Sarah, again touching glasses. '—y amor,' he added, eyes glinting.

'Salud,' murmured Sarah, her mouth dry. If her cheeks hadn't been pink already, the look in his eyes as he wished her love as well as health would have put colour there. He had the devil's own cheek, looking at her in that fashion in front of her grandmother. Not that Granny would object. She had seemed inordinately taken with him ever since he had claimed to be at her feet at the private view. If it weren't for Jamie's existence, she would be busy matchmaking, although to no purpose, did she but know it.

It looks as if I shall have to tell her what Kristen had to say about him, thought Sarah, her eyes downcast to avoid the caressing gleam of amusement in the sloe-black eyes of the man now stretched on the grass, supporting himself on one elbow.

'How many ponies do you keep here?' asked Mrs Grantham.

'Not as many as I once did. In my twenties polo was an obsession with me, in the same way that my father was an obsessive Crestarer. I was the black sheep of the family in those days . . . an idler, bent on enjoying life rather than doing anything useful. Now I try to combine the two,' he answered, crossing

one long booted leg over the other. 'By the way, my
cousin Mercedes, whose daughter I met at the airport,
is getting up a party to attend the first night of the
annual *feria* in Algeciras. Her husband is a relation of
the *alcalde*—the mayor—so they and their guests will
be sitting in a stand with an excellent view of the
carnival parade. If you'd care to join them, they'd be
delighted.'

'How very kind,' said Mrs Grantham. 'But I've
already accepted an invitation to see the parade from
the balcony of a flat of some English people who live
in Algeciras. But do thank your cousin for her invitation. I hear the parade is quite spectacular.'

Carlos laughed. 'It's actually rather a small town
affair compared with the fair at Seville. That's really
something. But Algeciras doesn't put on a bad show.
I'm sure you'll enjoy it.'

'It's a call from England for you. Jamie Drayton.'

Mrs Grantham vacated her armchair and passed
the receiver to Sarah.

Dressed and ready to leave for the *feria,* they were
waiting to be collected by some people from Puerto
de la Duquesa who were friends of their hosts and
were going to give them a lift to Algeciras and back.

Sarah's spontaneous reaction on being told it was
Jamie calling was a flicker of irritation that he should
have picked this particular moment to call her.

She had sent a couple of postcards to him since her
arrival, but had received nothing from him. Now here
he was on the telephone, at the most inconvenient
time he could have chosen, because at any moment
there would be a knock on the door and the unknown
couple would be expecting a welcome.

'Hello, Jamie. How are you?'

'I'm fine. Your second postcard came this morning. How are you?'

'Fine, thanks. Look, don't be offended if I have to ring off. Granny's expecting some visitors.'

'Oh . . . I see. Yes, okay. I understand. It sounds as if you're having marvellous weather. Much better than here. It hasn't stopped raining since you left.'

'Really? How miserable for you.'

'I've been thinking: if you had an extra week there, I could come down and join you. I could stay at the hotel rather than making extra work for your grand-mother.'

'Jamie, I don't think that's on,' said Sarah. 'I'm already booked for the motorail and it might not be easy to change dates.'

Tactfully, Mrs Grantham had disappeared into the kitchen. Hoping she couldn't hear this end of the conversation, Sarah added, 'And I'd rather not extend my visit . . . not at the moment.'

'Does that mean you've been missing me?' he asked, in a hopeful tone.

No, it means I want to get myself away from Carlos Hastings' orbit, was what she thought. Aloud, she said, 'I can hear voices in the entrance lobby . . . Granny's visitors are arriving. I'm sorry I can't talk now, but it's difficult to have a sensible conversation on long-distance anyway. It was nice of you to ring up.'

'I wanted to hear your voice. I miss you, Sarah . . . darling.' The endearment was tacked on uncertainly, wringing her heart with pity and guilt.

'Well, I'll be back very soon. Hope the rain's cleared up by then. I must go. Goodbye, Jamie.'

All they way to Algeciras, in the back of the Durhams' car, she felt fretted by his call and the suppliant tone of his voice. She found herself thinking that Carlos, in Jamie's position, wouldn't have rung up to ask if he could come down. He would have arrived on the doorstep and swept her into his arms.

That, of course, was the nub of the matter. In her daydreams about Jamie, she had invested him with a forceful and poetic ardour which in reality he lacked. He was a thoroughly nice man, but not an imaginative, irresistible lover for whose touch, after nine days apart, she now longed to the depths of her soul. And if she didn't feel like that now, before they were married, how was she going to feel after years of day-to-day living with him? And years of sleeping with him?

Perhaps it was only the not-nice men like Carlos Hastings who had the ability to make women tremble inwardly with no more than a mocking glance or a meaning word.

'——*y amor,*' he had murmured, smiling at her, instantly making her wonder how it would feel to be crushed to that muscle-armoured chest with his dark face poised above hers in the moment before he kissed her.

She wondered if she would see him at the *feria,* or if the grandstand erected for the mayor and his guests would be in one of the *plazas* rather than on the town's waterfront which was where her grandmother's friends had their apartment.

From the outside it was clear to see that Algeciras was *en fête.* The red and yellow Spanish flag was draped over many balconies. Side streets were hung with bunting. Families dressed in their best—many of the little girls wearing traditional dresses with flowers in their hair and make-up on their faces—were converging on the town centre. Not as many teenage and older girls were in costume, but those who were looked most attractive, their flounced skirts rippling

round their ankles, the long silky fringes of embroidered shawls swaying with each movement of their
arms. They brought an air of old Spain to a town
now largely rebuilt, although here and there a building
with windows protected by beautiful hand-wrought
rejas or a massive door still remained, lending charm
to the rather soulless designs of present-day Spanish
architects.

It was one of the modern buildings, its front faced
with ceramic tiles and its balconies railed with
aluminium, that the three women entered while Mr
Durham went in search of a parking space.

As the lift bore them up to the second floor, Sarah
thought how much more attractive Granny looked, in
her seventies, than Mrs Durham in her fifties. Mrs
Grantham was wearing a skirt of heavy white cotton
with a boat-necked black linen top and a string of
huge clear glass beads. With her brown skin and white
hair, the effect was simple yet chic. Mrs Durham's
flowered dress, however, did nothing for her full figure
and, being made of polyester, was obviously hot and
uncomfortable on a warm southern evening.

Sarah herself was wearing an aquamarine cotton
sun-dress with a matching jacket, an outfit she had
bought the year before for a school friend's summer
wedding. At the base of her throat lay a fine gold
chain with a pendant *S* resting in the hollow between
her collar-bones, and her ear-rings were small gold
knots, all three pieces of jewellery having been presents
from her brothers.

The interior of their hosts' flat was more pleasing
than the building of which it was part. Most of the
furniture was made of cane. Creamy-textured rugs
were spread over the floor. Closely-packed bookshelves
and paintings gave colour to the white walls.

But the flat's main charm was its spectacular view

across Algeciras harbour to the great Rock of
Gibraltar, still, at this time inaccessible because of the
closure of the frontier following a dispute between the
British and Spanish governments.

The hope that it would be re-opened before too
much longer was the subject of much speculation
among the guests at the party.

'Life will be so much easier when we can fly home
from Gib instead of having to go all the way to
Málaga,' Sarah was told by one man.

'And shop at Gib's Marks & Spencer,' chimed in
his wife.

Her remark reminded Sarah of the story Carlos had
told them about Mrs Violeta Buck, a woman who had
fallen in love with this country and embraced the
Spanish way of life. As I should if I lived here, she
thought.

Presently, a glass of wine in one hand and a small
sausage roll in the other, she wandered on to the
balcony to survey the scene on the esplanade on the
far side of the street below.

Several three-tiered stands of benches had been
erected on what were normally parking bays. One of
them must be the mayor's stand, she realised, with
quickening interest. There, seated on one of the chairs
installed for his most privileged guests, was Carlos's
cousin Mercedes. All the family were there except
Carlos.

The crowds lining both sides of the streets increased
as the time approached for the parade to begin.

'But it won't start on time. It never does. I've been
to countless parades in Spain—the arrival of the Three
Kings at Christmas and the penitents' processions at
Easter—and I've never known one to start punctually
yet,' someone told her disapprovingly.

It seemed to Sarah that it didn't much matter if the

parade was a little late starting as long as the sky remained clear. The people in the street appeared happy to chatter to friends and acquaintances while their children ate crisps and *caramelos* bought from passing vendors, or played with helium-filled silver balloons.

Of Carlos there was still no sign. As his relations hadn't kept a seat for him, she was forced to conclude that he wasn't coming. He had spoken slightly disparagingly of the parade, she remembered. Perhaps he had found something better to do . . . another more forthcoming girl to pursue, if indeed his attentions so far could be said to constitute a pursuit of her.

The daylight was beginning to fade when at last two policemen on motorbikes rode slowly into view, making sure the way was clear for the parade to follow them.

The sound of hooves clip-clopping on the hard surface of the road heralded the appearance of a group of horsemen, most of them dressed in tight waist-hugging trousers, short jackets and flat-brimmed felt hats. Several had girls in costume riding pillion. Many of their mounts were part-Arab, a reminder that from Algeciras it was only a short sea crossing to North Africa from whence had come the Moorish invasion of Spain and the fast agile Arab horses which had eventually superseded the chargers needed by horsemen encumbered by heavy armour.

Behind the main group came one man, riding alone. He was mounted on a grey Hispano, and he was dressed all in black except for his shirt which was white with small ruffles down the front of it. For a few moments, because his face was hidden by the tilted brim of his hat, Sarah didn't recognise him. Then she knew it was Carlos, and the wild lurch of her heart proved how dangerously vulnerable she had

become and how important it was to avoid any further
encounters with him.

As she watched his tall figure approach, one fist
resting on a lean hip, the other hand lightly cupping
the Hispano's reins, it became clear why he was riding
behind the rest of the cavalcade.

When he reached the far end of the *alcalde's* stand,
the Hispano began the Spanish walk, lifting his front
legs and extending them horizontally before putting
them down without bending his knees. He continued
to perform this air until, at the centre of the stand
where the mayor and his lady were sitting, Carlos
swept off his hat and bowed before starting to back-
rein the horse as far as the other end of the stand.

Sarah had never seen difficult paces performed with
such ease and perfection. She wasn't surprised when
horse and rider received bursts of applause at the end
of both feats.

Having completed his party piece, the grey resumed
a normal walk while his rider turned his attention to
the adjoining blocks of apartments on the inland side
of the roadway, scanning their balconies.

Could he be looking for her? Sarah wondered, half
inclined to draw back out of sight. But something held
her where she was, and moments later he spotted her,
or so she thought, and left the line of the procession
to cross to her side of the road.

It seemed she had been mistaken and it was actually
someone standing on the pavement under the balconies
who had attracted his attention. For a moment he
was lost to view unless she craned over to watch him.
When he reappeared, there was a dark red carnation
in his hand. She heard him say, *'Gracias, señora,'*
before he again looked up at the second floor balcony.
Touching the flower to his lips, with an expert flick of

the wrist he sent it spinning into the air for Sarah to catch.

The gallant gesture evoked laughter, applause and jocular cries of *'Olé!'* from the people in the street below, and exclamations of surprise and interest from Sarah's companions on the balcony. However, to her relief, the attention focused on her was short-lived, because the horses were followed by the first of the floats.

Behind them came a uniformed band with several girls in its ranks. The music was lively and loud enough to carry across the bay to La Línea, the town on the Spanish side of the border where lights were beginning to twinkle in the deepening twilight.

The parade went on for a long time, the atmosphere growing more festive as children in fancy dress on the floats pelted the watching crowds with flowers and streamers. Another band marched past, followed by a well-drilled team of high-stepping drum-majorettes. Folk dancers in Andalusian peasant costumes danced their way along the street. Then came a contingent of Guardia Civil in olive-green uniforms and shiny black hats.

'Used to be made of patent leather, but I'm told it's been replaced by plastic,' someone told Sarah.

Someone else had given her a pin to fasten the red carnation to the lapel of her jacket. She knew she would press it and keep it; a memento of a moment she would always remember even if the gesture had been an empty one, devoid of any significance other than a practised philanderer's understanding of the way to weaken feminine resistance.

The grand finale of the parade was a very large group of Rio-style carnival dancers, dressed in spectacular black and silver spider costumes, gyrating to South American rhythms.

By now, thought Sarah, as she watched them, the horsemen heading the parade must have been all round the town and have finished their part in the procession. She had heard that the *feria* would continue all night. It would be daylight again before the partying ended. But already several of the older people at *this* party were beginning to look fatigued. She knew the Durhams and her grandmother didn't intend to make a night of it.

As the spider dancers moved out of sight and the crowds streamed across the roadway, she saw that the mayor and his guests, including Carlos's relations, had disappeared. Perhaps they had gone to dine at a local restaurant.

She was in the sitting-room, helping to pass round sandwiches and cups of coffee, when the flat's doorbell rang. Her host went to answer it. The entrance hall being a small lobby with an arch opening into the sitting-room, most people present had a good view of the caller. There was a lull in the conversation as they recognised him.

'Good evening, sir.' Sarah, who had had her back to the door, drew in her breath and turned round. 'I'm hoping you're going to allow me to take away one of your guests,' said Carlos.

'By all means. Come in, young man. I certainly have no objection . . . if the lady hasn't. Here she is. Ask her,' the flat's owner suggested, with a chuckle.

There was now total silence as the other guests looked with interest at the tall black-clad man who looked like a Spaniard, rode like a Spaniard but spoke faultless English.

He advanced to where Sarah was standing, holding the plate of sandwiches.

'I thought you might like to see the informal side of the festivities . . . the booths where people meet old friends and make new ones. Nobody goes to bed on the first night of the *feria*. That's why it starts on a Saturday.'

'Thank you, but I don't think——' Sarah began, frantically searching her mind for a cast-iron excuse to decline an invitation she knew it would be madness to accept.

'Go on, lass. Go and enjoy yourself. You're too young and pretty to be stuck with a bunch of oldsters like us,' a male Lancashire voice said loudly from the other side of the room.

As everyone laughed and agreed, Sarah looked at her grandmother, hoping she might come to her rescue. To her dismay, Mrs Grantham's reaction to her silent appeal for help was to say, 'It sounds fun. But how will she get back, Carlos? Will you bring her or will there be taxis available? I'm getting a lift with some friends.'

'I'll bring Sarah back myself . . . but probably not before breakfast,' he added. Taking the plate of sandwiches from Sarah's hand and giving it to the person nearest to her, he asked, 'Have you a bag you want to bring with you?'

Seeing no way to extricate herself, short of a point-blank refusal which seemed likely to be overridden not only be Carlos but all these romantic old dears who had no idea what they might be letting her in for, she looked vaguely round for her small bag which she had put down somewhere.

It was spotted and handed round like pass-the-parcel until it reached her.

'Goodnight, everyone. *Adiós*.'

Taking her firmly by the elbow, Carlos propelled her to the door.

The silver Porsche sped through the moon-silvered countryside between Algeciras and Sotogrande, the only car on the winding ribbon of a road which began at Cadíz and went all the way round eastern Spain until at last it came to the great mountain range of the Pyrenees beyond which lay the rest of Europe.

Almería . . . Alicante . . . Valencia . . . Barcelona. The lovely musical names of some of the Spanish cities which lay between here and the faraway frontier with France sang in Sarah's mind as she sat in the passenger seat, watching the long golden beams of the powerful headlamps lighting up a stretch of road where a stand of tall old eucalyptus trees threw their black shadows across it now that the moon was no longer sailing high.

There were other names, of course, which conjured up less attractive images. Benidorm was one. That name was now synonymous with overcrowded beaches, hotels like battery houses, chips with everything, rowdy tourists getting drunk on cheap *vino*. But Benidorm wasn't typical of Spain any more than Blackpool was typical of England. According to Carlos, Benidorm and some of the resorts here on the Costa del Sol were unfortunate excrescences on the fair face of his mother's country.

Sarah glanced sideways at him. Although it was now four hours since he had come to the flat and virtually forced her into leaving with him, he still looked completely alert. Already a great deal of wine and hard liquor must have been drunk in Algeciras since the start of the week-long *feria*, but not very much had gone down her companion's throat.

He had had a few glasses of wine, but coffee and sometimes water had been his main drinks and no one had chaffed him about it or urged him to have something stronger. Among the people who knew him, he was obviously a popular figure and an admired one. Both sexes seemed to like him, so perhaps he confined his passes to foreigners like Kristen and herself and didn't chase Spanish women. Although she had noticed several pairs of dark eyes attempting to catch his tonight.

So far, she had to admit, he had not put a toe out of line as far as she was concerned. He couldn't have behaved more circumspectly if it had been the girl called Isabel whom he had been escorting. So far.

Sarah's earlier nervousness of him had revived when the time came to leave. After unlocking the car and watching her tuck her full skirt out of the way of the door, he had asked if she would like the passenger seat put in a reclining position.

'No, thank you,' she had said quickly. 'I'm not a bit tired. I expect I shall be later, but at the moment I'm wide awake.'

On the way out of town Carlos had slipped a cassette into the player. Sarah, after a night of music, dancing and the often loud voices of her fellow revellers, would have preferred silence. But when the tape started to play, it wasn't pop or flamenco but the familiar opening chords of one of her favourite piano concertos.

At first she found it relaxing to sit in luxurious comfort, looking out at the countryside by night and listening to the rippling cadenzas. The concerto was one which, in places, stirred her deepest emotions. After a while she began to wonder if somehow Carlos knew this and had chosen the music deliberately, to soften her up, as it were.

Again she looked furtively at him. Earlier, while they were dancing, he had removed the white bow tie he had worn for the parade and unbuttoned the neckband of his shirt. It was made of some fine white

fabric which, beautifully laundered, had kept its fresh-
ness in spite of the night's exertions. The small frills
and pin-tucks down the front served to emphasise the
masculinity of his looks; the forceful profile dramatic-
ally lit by the glow from the headlamps, the wide
shoulders under the black cloth, the strong hands
controlling the wheel.

The thought of those hands setting the brake,
switching off the engine and then reaching out to
touch her sent a *frisson* of mingled dread and excitement through her. She felt as nervous as if she had
never been kissed.

The entrance to the main part of the Sotogrande
development came before the side road leading past
the hotel and the flats. However, Sarah wasn't so
familiar with the road that as soon as Carlos eased
off the accelerator and, shortly after, changed down,
she guessed his intention. It was only when he began
to turn off at the gateway with the security booth that
it dawned on her where he was taking her.

' . . . *but probably not before breakfast,*' he had
added, after assuring her grandmother he would bring
Sarah back himself.

Breakfast was still hours away. There was plenty of
time to take her to his own house, bed her, and deliver
her to the flat before Mrs Grantham had set the table
on her jasmine-scented terrace.

The barrier was in its vertical position. Whether
there was a guard on duty in the booth as they swept
past, she didn't notice.

Her whole body suddenly tense, she said sharply,
'Where are we going?'

He glanced at her. *'Está tranquila!'*

She knew what it meant. Don't worry. Keep calm.

But the faint smile curling his mouth did nothing
to allay the panic she felt rising in her.

CHAPTER THREE

'You said you weren't tired,' Carlos reminded her, as the car swept along the main road through the development.

'I wasn't . . . then. I am now. I—I think I should go home and catch up a few hours' sleep.' Sarah tried to sound calm and firm rather than rattled.

She had been expecting him to kiss her. That had seemed unavoidable. But an embrace in the car when they reached the flats would have been easy to cope with—or so it seemed now—compared with being taken to his house and there . . .

Sarah's mind recoiled from the unpleasant prospect of having to resist a determined attempt to persuade her to go to bed with him.

'What I have in mind is the perfect conclusion to a night at the *feria*,' he told her. 'If the drive back has made you drowsy, you'll soon find yourself waking up and recovering your energy. There'll be plenty of time for sleeping later. Right now there are better things to do.'

He spoke in the tone of someone who has decided on a course and won't be easily deflected from it. The trouble was Sarah was not at all sure she could deflect him—or wished to. He was the most compelling man she had ever met. Even if, to him, she was merely one of a long line of conquests, to her he was someone special—*almost* the complete embodiment of all she admired in the opposite sex.

Would it be so very wrong to go along with his

'perfect conclusion' to this already unforgettable night? Other girls did this kind of thing and thought nothing of it. Who was going to know or care if for once in her life she kicked over the traces?

Jamie would care.

At the realisation of how completely she had forgotten him, even though it was less than twelve hours since they had spoken on the telephone, she felt ashamed; and even more ashamed of being tempted to give herself to a man who cared nothing for her.

'I'd like to go home, please,' she said, in a resolute voice.

'Well . . . if you insist,' he responded, with obvious reluctance.

'I do,' she affirmed, feeling both foolish and determined.

No doubt he thought her a prude and a waste of the time he had spent on her, but she couldn't help that.

'Very well . . . but I should have thought you'd enjoy a walk along the beach and watching the sun rise. It's one of my favourite times of day . . . first light.' He reduced the car's speed and steered it closer to the verge, preparatory to making a U-turn.

'Oh . . . ' she said. 'Oh . . . well, yes . . . perhaps it is a good idea to have some fresh air. All right, I'll come with you.'

Carlos changed gear and increased speed. 'I gather you thought I had something different in mind,' he said drily.

'You knew what I thought,' she retorted. 'In fact you encouraged me to think it.' She saw now that he had been teasing her ever since her first anxious 'Where are we going?'

'Mm, perhaps I did,' he agreed. 'But you didn't need much encouragement, did you? I've sensed that

you're wary of me since our first meeting. Why is
that? Because I'm half Spanish? Because I'm older
than your usual boy-friends?'

She didn't dispute the truth of his statement.
'Perhaps those things have something to do with it,
but mainly it's your reputation.' As soon as she had
spoken, she regretted the unguarded remark.

There was a long pause. She wondered what he was
thinking. By now they were approaching the colony
of flats and cottages surrounding the Sotogrande beach
club. Driving slowly to make as little noise as possible,
Carlos tucked the car into a parking bay not far from
the beach itself.

As she had imagined him doing, a short time ago,
he switched off, set the handbrake and removed the
key from the ignition. But his next act wasn't to reach
for her.

Unclipping his belt and turning sideways in his seat,
he said, 'My reputation isn't a good one, I gather?
What have you heard about me?'

The unwisdom of what she had said made her fidget
with the cord of her bag. After considering various
answers, she settled for, 'Only that you don't take
women very seriously.'

He wasn't going to let her off the hook. 'What is
that supposed to mean?'

'That you're looking for playmates rather than a
wife, I imagine. Perhaps you've already tried marriage
and didn't like it,' she added.

'No, I've never been married. So far a permanent
partner hasn't seemed necessary,' he replied. 'Perhaps
I shall change my mind about that one of these days,
but my observation of other people's marriages isn't
encouraging.'

'Your parents were happy together, weren't they?'

'To the best of my recollection, yes—extremely. But

nine years isn't long. Had they lived, they might have split up later.'

'That's a very cynical view.'

'I am a cynic . . . and have reason to be. Come on, let's get some sea air in our lungs. You can't walk on sand in those heels. Leave your shoes and your bag in the car.'

He opened the driver's door and swung his long legs out of the car before tugging off his jodhpur-style boots and black silk socks.

Where it marched with the ornamental gardens in the centre of the low blocks of flats, the shore was a wide slope of sand lapped by a flat calm sea. As they walked towards the water's edge, Carlos paused to turn up the bottoms of his trousers. Cut close to the leg like the regimental dress trousers Sarah remembered her father wearing when she was a little girl, they could be folded no higher than just above the ankle bones. His feet were as brown as his hands, she noticed. No doubt his house had a swimming pool where, like her, he had soaked up the sun.

By this time the moon was sinking towards the hills in the hinterland and the stars had become faint pinpricks. But even away from the lamps in the gardens there was still enough light to see the sand and the water, and one or two beached fishing boats. The sea here wasn't tidal, she knew. Without a wind to whip up breakers, there was no rhythmic ebb and flow to remind her of the childhood holidays when she and her mother had prospected for pebbles and shells along the foreshore of English beaches.

'What time does the sun rise?' she asked.

'In about half an hour. There are some rocks further along where we can sit and watch it come up . . . if you're not cold.'

'Not at all.'

For much of the night she had dispensed with her jacket, dancing with her shoulders bare except for the narrow straps which were decorative, not a support for the bodice of her sun-dress. It was lined with batiste and cleverly shaped to obviate the need for a strapless bra when the wearer, like Sarah, had firm breasts. Until they were driving home, she hadn't been conscious of being scantily clad. But in the car she had realised that, for a practised seducer, it would be the work of seconds to push aside the thin straps and whip down the zip at the back, leaving her top half accessible to his exploring hands.

At his question the thought returned of how it would feel to be touched by those lean brown fingers which, no doubt, had long been expert in giving pleasure to partners more willing than she. For she still wasn't sure if he *had* been teasing her. It could have been a try-on.

If the 'perfect conclusion' had been what she thought he had meant, and she hadn't insisted on being taken home, would they be walking by the sea, or would they be in his bedroom? How would she ever know?

She was thinking about being kissed by him when, suddenly, he took her by the arm, making her come to a standstill, making her think he was going to kiss her, here and now.

Instead he said, 'That carnation has wilted. Let me get rid of it for you.'

Before she could speak, he had unpinned the flower from her jacket and tossed it into the sea where it would soon become waterlogged and disappear.

The act struck her as symbolic. By his own admission, to him women were like flowers. He enjoyed them, but only for a short time. Soon they were discarded like the dark red carnation floating on the surface of the sea.

'Your holiday will soon be over,' he remarked, as they moved on. 'How will you go about finding a new job?'

'There's a magazine called *The Lady* which is always full of advertisements for mothers' helps and professional nannies. It's no problem getting a job now that so many women have careers which prevent them from taking more than a short maternity leave if they want to keep their place in the business world, or wherever they operate. I'll probably be employed again within a fortnight of getting back. Unless I try for an overseas post. That might take longer to fix.'

A few steps further on, she added, 'I can see that a wife may not be necessary to you, but what about children? I thought bankers were like royalty; they needed children to take over from them and keep the business in the family.'

'That is so, but my English cousins have already been quite prolific and are hoping I'll leave it to them to keep the line going,' he said drily. 'I certainly don't plan to marry merely to perpetuate my branch of the family. Do you look forward to having children of your own, or has minding other people's brats doused your maternal instinct?'

'I don't think of children as brats. If they are, it's the fault of the adults in charge of them. A maternal instinct—except in the general sense of feeling protective towards all very young creatures—seems to me something which doesn't come into action until a girl finds a man she would like to be the father of her children,' Sarah answered.

'And you haven't met him yet, I gather?'

To reply, 'I'm not sure' would be to invite questions in which he had no real interest and she didn't want to answer. It was simplest to say baldly, 'No.'

'You're not so much older than Isabel,' said Carlos.

'There's plenty of time for marriage later. If I were a woman, I'd want to spend most of my twenties and possibly longer enjoying my independence. Even today, marriage usually changes a woman's life more than it does a man's. I think women are like horses. The later a horse is put to work, the sounder it is in maturity. It's the same with women and marriage.'

'That was a splendid animal you were riding in the parade. You're a brilliant horseman,' she told him impulsively. She had meant to compliment him sooner.

'*Gracias.*' He gave a slight bow, an un-English gesture which went with the clothes he was wearing. After a pause, he added, 'Yes, even my detractors, of whom there are many, including the one you've encountered, would allow that I ride well. But as I was put on a pony before I could walk and rode every day with my mother, here and in England, it would be surprising if I didn't. On the whole I find horses more *simpático* than people. They never have ulterior motives.'

His cynical streak was showing again, making her wonder what experiences had moulded his outlook.

The sky was beginning to glow with light from beyond the horizon. When they came to the rocks he had mentioned, Carlos took off his jacket and spread it for her to sit on.

'Will you be warm enough without it?' she asked, looking at the thin lawn of his shirt, so fine she could see his brown skin and flat dark nipples. Unlike the Spanish men she had seen using the hotel pool, he wasn't noticeably hairy.

He nodded and walked away to pick up a large flat pebble and throw it at the surface of the sea, which it hit and bounced off three times. Sarah watched him repeat the action, the tight black trousers accentuating the lines of his long legs and hard male backside.

It was Carlos, not the brightening sky, she wanted
to go on looking at. But she forced her gaze upwards
to where streaks of luminous colour, apricot, rose and
gold, presaged the sunrise. It seemed to come out of
the sea, a great glowing ball of fire, too bright to be
looked at directly.

'It's easy to understand why ancient cultures
worshipped the sun, isn't it?' she said, as he came
back to the rocks and sat down, not sharing the jacket
he had spread for her but choosing another flat rock
more than an arm's length away.

Once in view, the sun seemed to rise more quickly
so that within a few minutes the roseate sky had
disappeared and another golden Andalusian morning
was beginning.

'Your grandmother will probably oversleep. Why
not come back to my house and have a swim and
some coffee?' Carlos suggested. 'There are several
bikinis in the pool pavilion. I'm sure one of them will
fit you.'

It was a tempting suggestion, but what might it lead
to? It wasn't only by moonlight that a girl could get
carried away.

Sarah shook her head. 'I think I ought to get back
and take Granny breakfast in bed.'

He wasn't deceived by her excuse. 'You still don't
trust me, do you?'

She gave him a level look. 'Should I?'

He looked amused. 'Perhaps not. Although I've
never found it necessary to force my attentions on
anyone, if that's what's worrying you.'

Which isn't to say that you'd never coax someone
into acting against her better judgment, she thought.

'I'm sure you haven't . . . and equally sure that
girls like Isabel don't visit bachelors' houses without
some form of chaperonage,' she answered. 'When in

Rome, you know.' She stood up and shook out his jacket. 'What happened to your horse? Where is he now?'

'Back in his stable at my house. He was brought home in a box by my groom, José-Maria, whose grandfather looked after my grandfather's horses. Did you know there was a hunt in this area? The Guadiaro Hunt. San Enrique de Guadiaro is a village a few kilometres off the main road.'

Sarah said, 'How unexpected! I've never hunted. Have you?'

'I go out with them occasionally. It was started in the late Seventies by an English couple. The hounds—beagles—were brought from England. It's a drag hunt . . . nothing to upset the anti-blood-sports faction.'

'I can never make up my mind about hunting. I'm inclined to feel that if Prince Charles, who is such a civilised man with his butterfly garden and his interest in alternative medicine . . . if he hunts, the pros must outweigh the cons.'

'So Prince Charles is your *beau idéal*, is he?'

'They both are. Don't you think she's lovely?'

She wondered if, in spite of his propensities, he might still have an ideal woman, perhaps based on his memories of his beautiful mother. Surely she must have been a beauty if his father had fallen headlong in love with her and, together, they had produced an extraordinarily attractive son?

'She's a charming girl,' Carlos agreed. 'But whether she loved him for himself or because of the glamour which surrounded him as a future king, and the life she would enjoy as Princess of Wales, who can say?'

'I'm sure she loved him for himself,' was Sarah's rather indignant reaction. 'That's carrying your cynicism too far. It's obvious that she adores him.'

'She may also adore a virtually unlimited clothes allowance and the many other perks of the job,' he responded sardonically.

'I don't believe it. I doubt if she gave that a thought. She was just a young girl in love with a super guy,' she retorted vehemently.

His attitude made her so angry that she broke into a jog, not sure if he was deliberately trying to rile her or if he believed his allegation. Either way, she was in danger of losing her temper. A run would act as a safety-valve and stop her blowing up.

The sand by the water's edge was firm underfoot and Sarah was in good shape from long swims in the pool and country walks. Without glancing behind her, she couldn't tell if Carlos was continuing to stroll or if he was keeping pace a short way behind her.

After jogging a few hundred yards, she began to calm down. It was rare for her to feel as angry as she had a few minutes before. She couldn't remember the last time she had come close to boiling point. But with Carlos all her emotions seemed keyed to a fine pitch, all her senses abnormally sensitive.

As she approached the beach flats, she turned away from the sea to head in a diagonal line for the place where they had left the car. The slope of the beach and the softer sand slowed her down. As she was reducing speed, she felt a sudden sharp pain in the ball of one foot, enough to make her stumble and fall.

She had twisted into a sitting position and was staring with dismay at the bright blood dribbling from a deep cut when Carlos reached her.

He went down on his knees and picked up her foot by the ankle to examine the injury.

'Glass!' he said succinctly. 'Have you got a handkerchief or tissues on you?'

The skirt of her dress had a pocket in the side seam, but there was nothing in it.

'In my bag in the car. Not here.'

'Neither have I. Anyway, it will take more than a handkerchief to soak up this.'

Placing her heel on the sand, he sat back on his own heels and began to undo his shirt buttons.

'You can't use your shirt,' she protested.

'It may not be as hygienic as a sterilised dressing, but in an emergency one has to use what's to hand. If that foot isn't bound up, you'll get blood on your dress and on the carpet in the car,' he answered. 'Whoever is supposed to be keeping this beach in order is doing a poor job. I'll have to speak to someone about it.'

As he spoke, he tugged his shirt out of his trousers and quickly stripped it off.

The sight of his splendid torso, caramel-brown and rippling with muscle, effectively took Sarah's mind off her bleeding foot and the ruination of his expensive shirt. In fact Carlos didn't rip it into pieces as she had anticipated, but first wiped away the reddened sand caking her sole and then used the body of the shirt to pad the cut, binding it in place with the sleeves.

'There . . . that should do for the time being.'

Before she knew what he was about, he put his jacket on her lap and scooped her off the sand as easily as if she weighed no more than a saddle.

As he walked up the beach with her cradled against his bare chest, one strong arm supporting her back, the other beneath her legs, Sarah's heart seemed to turn over and she felt other sensations which she recognised as a far more overpowering reaction than she had ever experienced in Jamie's arms. For the few minutes it took for them to reach the Porsche, every nerve in her body seemed to quiver with a primitive longing to be swept off her feet in every sense.

At the car, he set her down on her good foot while he unlocked the passenger door.

'Before you swing your legs inside, I'll get a towel from the boot and give that foot another wrapping. Is it hurting much?'

'Not yet. I can hardly feel it.'

'You will later, I expect.'

Returning from the rear of the car with a beach towel, he enfolded her foot in it, saying, 'Rather than alarming your grandmother, who may not have a proper first-aid kit, we'll go to my place. Don't worry: you won't be alone with me—Amparo is there. She was my mother's nursemaid, then mine, and now she's my housekeeper here.'

Five minutes later a pair of electronically-controlled gates were slowly swinging apart to allow the car to pass between them. Even when the gates were open, little could be seen from the roadway as the drive was bordered on both sides by dense and tall cypress hedges.

Where one hedge ended, the car swung left and entered a large gravelled forecourt with space to park several cars and garaging for three vehicles built as a wing projecting from the main structure of a one-storey house. The high wall surrounding the grounds and the dark green hedge screening the drive formed the other sides of the forecourt. The wall of the house was pierced by a solid-looking door flanked by two small and heavily barred windows, but was otherwise blank. The effect was severe and unwelcoming. There were not even tubs of geraniums to soften the impression of a house built to shut out the world and guard its owner's seclusion.

As he brought the car to a halt alongside the door, Carlos pipped the horn. Then he got out and came round to help Sarah. She held the towel round her foot as she swivelled sideways, relieved to see that no drop of her blood had leaked through the makeshift wrappings to mar the pale grey wool pile with which the Porsche was fitted.

'There's no need to carry me. I can hobble,' she said, as he helped her to stand.

'It's quicker and easier to carry you.'

He had just picked her up when the front door opened. A small woman appeared. She was wearing a dark print dress with a clean apron tied over it. Her hair was scraped back in a bun. Like every Spanish female from babies in arms to ancient black-clad widows, she had pierced ears and wore small pearl studs.

'*Ah . . . qué pasa?*' she exclaimed, seeing at once that something was wrong.

Carlos explained briefly what had happened, then he introduced them.

Amparo stood aside while he carried Sarah into a hall with several open doors leading off it. The hall had larger windows on its inner side, but curtains were drawn across them, and the surrounding rooms were also curtained. Not all light was excluded, but for anyone coming in from the bright morning outside it was too dark to see the furnishings and pictures clearly.

With a touch of impatience in his voice, Carlos said something to his housekeeper who, after closing the outer door, was now hurrying ahead of them.

'As soon as I'm out of the way she follows the Spanish custom of excluding almost all light,' he told Sarah. 'In July and August, the hot months, it does help to keep the house cool. But for the rest of the year I prefer to admit the sun, even if it does fade the rugs and covers. I'll attend to your foot in my bathroom.'

To get there they had to cross his bedroom. The bed looked even bigger than king-size, with a green and gold carved and painted headboard which looked as it if might have come from his grandfather's *castillo*. That and a wall of books was all Sarah had time to notice before they entered the bathroom.

It was as large as the average bedroom and decorated in a style that was more international than Spanish. There was an armchair, covered in green and white cotton to match the curtains, which on Carlos's instructions Amparo pushed close to the bidet.

He then lowered Sarah into the chair where she was able to sit comfortably while he made the beach towel into a pad to support her leg with her foot hanging over the centre of the bidet.

Amparo gave a shocked exclamation when Carlos unwrapped his shirt and tossed it into the nearby bath. But whether she was horrified at his shirt being spoiled or by the amount of blood their visitor had shed, it was hard to say.

While Carlos was washing his hands and giving his nails a good scrub before attending to the wound, the housekeeper left the bathroom for a few moments and returned with a short-sleeved linen sports shirt for him.

After asking her to make some coffee for the *señorita*, he put the shirt on, saying to Sarah, 'She has strict ideas about what is proper and improper. Bare skin is acceptable by the pool but nowhere else. You'd think after years in the service of a reprobate such as myself she would have relaxed her ideas!'

Although it was said to tease her, the thought had already struck Sarah that a housekeeper who saw impropriety in a man stripped to the waist in the presence of a female visitor was unlikely to have stayed on his staff if the huge bed in the next room was frequently shared by young women.

By the time Amparo returned he had produced a well-stocked first-aid box and had cleaned and disinfected the wound in a manner suggesting it wasn't the first minor injury he had dealt with.

The Spanish woman placed her tray on the counter of veined apricot marble surrounding the handbasin. She asked Carlos how his guest liked her coffee.

'*Con leche . . . sin azúcar,*' he replied, without consulting Sarah.

While Amparo was filling two cups, he said, 'The gash isn't so large it will need a stitch, but a tetanus jab might be advisable. Or are you up to date on your shots?'

'I had a booster quite recently. I'm in the clear for five years.'

'Good.' He started to dress the wound. 'I'm afraid this is going to stop you swimming until it's healed. You may even have to postpone your return to England. You can't drive with a painful cut on the ball of your clutch foot.'

'Oh, I hope not!' she exclaimed.

'As you're not employed at the moment, I should have thought you'd be glad of an excuse to spend some more time in the sun,' he remarked, glancing at her.

'It isn't vital for me to get back,' she agreed. 'But I'd rather return as planned. It's very nice staying with Granny, but I do need to work for my living. My father isn't a rich man. He can't afford to support me indefinitely—in fact he and my stepmother have a problem making ends meet. They might seem to be comfortably off, but in fact they're rather hard-pressed.'

But what would Carlos, a scion of one of Europe's great banking dynasties, know about the financial problems of a man like her father? she thought. And although it might not be vital for her to get back, it *was* vital for her to leave Sotogrande as soon as possible.

Even though, at present, the touch of his fingers was as impersonal as that of a doctor, the effect on her told her how dangerously close to falling in love with him she was. To prolong her stay could only increase that danger, and the risk of having her life blighted by an obviously hopeless passion for a man who would never have serious feelings about her.

The fact had to be faced that she wasn't in his league. Men like Carlos married for other reasons than love. They chose their wives from among the daughters of their peers; girls brought up in the same world of inherited wealth and power.

A children's nanny, the daughter of a retired Army officer impoverished by inflation and struggling to keep up a style of life long out of date, had no chance. Especially as she wasn't a beauty, but only a passably attractive girl who had caught his eye at a time when beauties were in short supply.

Amparo handed her the coffee and nodded approvingly at the efficient way Carlos was binding the dressing in place with a crêpe bandage. Then she turned her attention to the shirt in the bath. Putting the plug in the waste pipe, she ran the cold tap, muttering to herself.

'She says that as the blood hasn't had time to set, the shirt should be as good as new by tomorrow,' Carlos translated.

'I hope so. I'd hate to have ruined it.'

'I have others,' he said, with a shrug. 'It was more important to protect your dress from bloodstains. I like dresses which fit at the waist and have full skirts. So many of the clothes girls are wearing at the moment are shapeless and unfeminine. I prefer girls to look like girls.'

He secured the bandage with a safety-pin. Then, Amparo still being bent over the bath, swishing the shirt about in the cold water, he ran his hand lightly up Sarah's leg as far as the knee, which he gave a soft squeeze.

'There you are. Now, while you're drinking your coffee, I'll go and call your grandmother and tell her what's happened, and that I'll bring you home after breakfast. Don't put your foot on the floor or try standing on it. If you do, it will re-start the bleeding. It needs to be kept elevated for the rest of the day if you want it to heal quickly.'

Sarah did as she was told. As she sipped the hot coffee, from the other room she could hear him dialling her grandmother's number. Would Mrs Grantham be awake yet after a late night? Evidently she was. A few seconds later he was explaining the situation to her.

Listening, Sarah thought that even his voice was fatally attractive. It was one of those distinctive, once-heard-forever-recognisable voices. With his height, looks, voice and charismatic personality, he could have made a career in the theatre or politics, she thought.

He came back. 'She'll expect us when she sees us. Now I suggest you take a couple of pain-killers before your foot starts to throb, and then we'll have breakfast on the terrace.'

At the back of the house was a garden of such unexpected beauty compared with the forbidding entrance that, momentarily, Sarah's surprise took her mind off being in his arms for the third time.

The garden surrounded a large Roman swimming

pool with a springboard at the deep end and steps
leading out of the shallow end to the paved deck in
front of the changing pavilion which had Moorish
arches wreathed in white bougainvillaea. All the flowers
in the garden were white. Great swags of white roses.
Tubbed white azaleas. Borders of white agapanthus.
Walls veiled by clouds of white jasmine.

Squabs with pale blue linen covers which wouldn't
be left out all night had already been placed on a sun-
bed with a white cane table beside it. Sarah guessed
that this was where Carlos sat every morning after the
early swim which was part of his fitness programme.

'Don't let me stop you having your usual dip,' she
said, as he placed her on the cushions.

'I'll swim later.' He went into a store alongside the
two changing-rooms and came out with a director-
style chair for himself to sit on.

'What an exquisite garden! Granny would be green
with envy. She made the most lovely garden at Las
Golondrinas which she claims not to miss, but I'm
sure she does. It had a stream running through it,'
said Sarah. 'Oh . . . dolphins!'

Her eye had been caught by a piece of sculpture set
on a plinth at the far corner of the pool. It was a
flight of three dolphins, cast in a gleaming silvery
metal which gave them the sleek wet sheen of real
dolphins leaping out of water.

Carlos had not yet sat down. Before doing so he
moved away to touch one of a bank of switches on
the wall of the pavilion. Instantly three shining jets of
water issued from the dolphins' smiling mouths to
form plumes of crystal drops above the transparent
depths of the pool.

'I saw the original sculpture in America and
commissioned a smaller version,' he told her. 'It looks
even better at night when the underwater lights are

on. In the past few years I've found myself buying more sculptures than paintings. Are you interested in art?'

'Yes . . . but I'm not at all knowledgeable,' she hastened to add.

She was rather surprised that art should be one of his interests. It didn't seem to go with polo. Perhaps he was like his house; keeping an intellectual side concealed behind the sporting, womanising façade.

The sun-bed had thick rubber wheels and wooden handles at its foot. Carlos wheeled her around the garden to look at some other sculptures, modern and antique. Then Amparo appeared with a trolley bearing their breakfast.

'Do you always have champagne for breakfast?' asked Sarah, when she noticed that on the lower shelf of the trolley was an ice-bucket with a foil-wrapped green bottle in it.

'Always on Sundays or special days, or after a night without sleep. Today qualifies on all three counts. It's the best possible reviver for flagging energy.'

'You don't look as if your energy ever flagged,' she remarked, wondering about the nights without sleep and why today counted as special.

'It doesn't often,' he agreed. 'Perhaps what happened to my parents has made me understand the importance of packing one's life as full of pleasures as possible. I try to live as if there were no tomorrow . . . which there may not be. *Quién sabe?*'

She knew what that meant. Who knows?

Breakfast consisted of the same chewy local brown bread which her grandmother bought in long pointed crusty rolls, with strong-flavoured Spanish butter and a thick amber jam, made by Amparo, which Carlos said was called angel's hair. There was also a basket of fruit, a large pot of coffee and another of hot milk.

'Mm . . . this is bliss,' murmured Sarah, licking her lips after sampling Amparo's jam. 'I'm sure if the Reverend Sydney Smith had eaten a champagne breakfast, in the sun, in a Spanish garden, to the sound of a fountain, he would have revised his definition of heaven as "eating *pâté de foie gras* to the sound of trumpets". He sounds such a civilised man. He can't have known what they do to geese to fatten their livers, poor things. I couldn't eat it. Could you?'

'I have eaten it in the past. I don't any more,' Carlos conceded. 'But I use leather tack and wear leather boots and belts, so my scruples are inconsistent. Would you spurn a fur coat if one were given to you?'

'A new fur coat—yes, I should. Not old furs. Edwardian sables or a silver fox cape from the Thirties.'

A telephone rang in the house. He said, 'Excuse me,' and rose.

While he was gone, Sarah sipped her champagne and thought about living each day as if there were no tomorrow.

She knew that, if she could be certain this *was* the last day of her life, when Carlos came back she would say, 'You are the most gorgeous man I have ever met. If you want me, I'm yours. Take me. Make love to me.'

There were girls with the courage to do that, but she wasn't one of them. Only the most desperate circumstances could overcome her innate belief that declarations of that sort were a male prerogative. Carlos would never know how easily, with a little more persistence, she would have succumbed to him.

'Goodbye, darling. It's been lovely having you here.

Come again soon.' Molly Grantham gave her favourite grandchild a farewell hug and kissed her on both cheeks. 'And don't forget to give me a buzz, as you young things say, when you get to Madrid tomorrow morning.'

'I won't,' Sarah promised. 'Goodbye, Granny. Thank you for having me. It's been a super holiday.'

A few minutes later she was driving away, sticking her arm out of the window to give a final wave to the slim white-haired figure she could see in her rear-view mirror.

That her grandmother didn't depend on visits from her family to relieve the loneliness of her life as a widow was a comforting thought. From now until the autumn, most of the flats would be occupied, either by their owners or people renting them; and having the use of the hotel's facilities made a big difference to Granny's life. She couldn't be in a better set-up for an elderly woman on her own, was Sarah's reflection as she turned the car on to the main road to Algeciras.

Fortunately the injury to her foot hadn't taken long to heal. It still gave the odd twinge and she couldn't run on it yet, but depressing the clutch didn't hurt and it hadn't been necessary to postpone the date of her departure.

As she drove past the main entrance to the Sotogrande estate, it was impossible not to think of the man whose disturbing image she had tried to banish from her mind since last seeing him two days ago.

He had been on his way to a party in Marbella and had called at the flat, looking heartbreakingly handsome in a white dinner jacket. He hadn't said a final farewell and she had expected him to call again, as he had every day since her accident. But that had been the last she had seen of him, and she was forced to conclude that he was now involved with some girl he had met at the party and she, Sarah, was forgotten.

When, last night, she had expressed this thought to her grandmother, Mrs Grantham had disagreed.

'Carlos has impeccable manners. I'm sure he wouldn't not bother to say goodbye if he realised you were leaving tomorrow. Perhaps he has got the date muddled, or he may have been busy today and intends to come round in the morning.'

But he hadn't come and Sarah had resisted her grandmother's urging to ring him up.

'If he were a different sort of man, I would. But he'll think I'm chasing him . . . hoping he'll ask for my telephone number in England,' she had said.

'When he finds out you've gone, he may ask me for it.'

'I doubt it.'

She hadn't said so to her grandmother, but privately Sarah felt sure she had been dropped, in Kristen's phrase, like a hot potato. Not because Carlos guessed she was dangerously close to falling in love with him, but because he had known since bringing her back from the *feria* that she wasn't a fun-and-games girl and had only continued to visit her until he met someone who was.

Nevertheless, although she had no illusions about the man, she couldn't help feeling a pang as she passed the road to his house and knew it was most unlikely she would ever set eyes on him again.

The railway station at Algeciras was at the back of the town but not far from the shopping centre. Between handing over the car to be loaded on to the auto express and boarding the Talgo herself, Sarah planned to buy cigars for her father and a present for Harriet. If she couldn't find anything suitable, there would be another opportunity in Madrid tomorrow. She would have the whole day to explore the capital before continuing to Paris tomorrow night.

At least I'm going home with my mind made up about Jamie, she thought, slowing down to follow a lorry along a bendy stretch of road.

She knew now with absolute certainty that she couldn't marry him. Carlos had proved that to her. She wouldn't have been violently attracted to him if she had loved Jamie with all her heart. It was as simple as that. She hadn't acknowledged it to herself at the time, but from the moment Carlos had scooped her off the beach, holding her close to his heart and making hers flutter as wildly as a trapped bird, deep down she had known she could never be Jamie's wife.

He had been her first love and would always be dear to her. But somewhere along the way she had fallen out of love with him. It was sad, and she hated having to hurt him, but it couldn't be avoided. She would tell him as soon as she got back.

Algeciras was still bedecked for the *feria*. When, having left her overnight case in the care of a porter, Sarah walked to the shops, she discovered they were closed. She had enough Spanish to ask a passerby what time they would re-open after the siesta, and was told that during the *feria* they were open only in the morning.

Unable to shop, Sarah strolled to the waterfront. Here and there remnants of coloured paper streamers still littered the esplanade, reminding her of the parade and of Carlos throwing the carnation up to the balcony. How long would it take to forget him? For forget him she must.

On her way back to the station, nearly there, she was waiting to cross the road when suddenly, in the stream of passing traffic, she saw the silver Porsche.

As it went by, Carlos smiled at her. He then drove
into the station yard.

Had her grandmother been right? Had he not
realised she was leaving today, discovered his mistake
and come all this way to say goodbye to her?

Forcing herself not to run to catch him up, not to
show the excitement and pleasure she felt at the sight
of him, she crossed the road and walked at an unhur-
ried pace to where he had stopped the car and was
climbing out of it.

'So you were going to leave without saying goodbye
to me,' was his first remark, as she came up to him.
'That wasn't very friendly, was it?'

'I thought you were being unfriendly not coming to
say goodbye to me,' she countered.

'I knew it wasn't necessary.'

'What do you mean?'

'I'm also taking the Talgo tonight. We shall be
travelling companions. I thought you might like to
have an interpreter and guide on your day in Madrid,
so I changed my departure date. I'm in a no-parking
area. Let me get rid of the car and then we'll go and
have a drink in the hotel across the road—it's pleas-
anter there than in the station buffet.'

He got back inside the Porsche and drove away to
deliver it into the hands of the loaders.

Stunned by this turn of events, Sarah stood where
he had left her, her mind in a whirl. Part of her was
thrilled that he'd changed his plans to travel with her.
But she couldn't help wondering what state her heart
would be in by the time they reached Paris.

FIRST-CLASS ROMANCE

Mail This Heart TODAY!

And We'll Deliver:

4 FREE BOOKS
A FREE MANICURE SET
PLUS
A SURPRISE MYSTERY BONUS
TO YOUR DOOR!

HARLEQUIN®DELIVERS FIRST-CLASS ROMANCE— DIRECT TO YOUR DOOR

Mail the Heart sticker on the postpaid order card today and you'll receive:

—4 new Harlequin Presents novels—FREE
—a beautiful manicure set—FREE
—and a surprise mystery bonus—FREE

But that's not all. You'll also get:

Money-Saving Home Delivery

When you subscribe to Harlequin Presents, the excitement, romance and faraway adventures of these novels can be yours for previewing in the convenience of your own home at less than retail prices. Every month we'll deliver 8 new books right to your door. If you decide to keep them, they'll be yours for only $2.24 each. That's 26¢ less per book than you would pay in a store—plus 89¢ for postage and handling per shipment.

Special Extras—FREE

Because our home subscribers are our most valued readers, we'll be sending you additional free gifts from time to time as a token of our appreciation.

OPEN YOUR MAILBOX TO A WORLD OF LOVE AND ROMANCE EACH MONTH. JUST COMPLETE, DETACH AND MAIL YOUR FREE OFFER CARD TODAY!

You'll love your beautiful manicure set—
an elegant and useful accessory, compact
enough to carry in your handbag. Its rich
burgundy case is a perfect expression of
your style and good taste—and it's yours
free with this offer!

Remember! To receive your free books, manicure set and mystery gift, return the postpaid card below. But don't delay!

DETACH AND MAIL CARD TODAY.

If offer card has been removed, write to: Harlequin Reader Service, P.O. Box 609, Fort Erie, Ontario L2A 5X3

CHAPTER FOUR

ALTHOUGH she had had no qualms about travelling alone, even with her limited Spanish, it was nice to be under the wing of someone who by his mere presence seemed to command instant and attentive service, thought Sarah, as they left the Hotel Octavio to return to the station.

'What sort of soldiers are those young men with red tassels on their caps?' she asked, seeing a group of them, laden with kitbags and grips, leaving the station yard and taking the road to the harbour.

'They're *legionarios* in the Spanish Foreign Legion going back to their base at Ceuta on the other side of the Straits,' Carlos told her.

Inside the station building quite a number of people who had come from the Moroccan side of the Straits of Gibraltar were waiting to board the Talgo; men in caftans with embroidered skullcaps and women in long robes with scarves hiding their hair.

'I rather regret not taking the day trip to Tangier while I was here,' said Sarah, as she and Carlos followed the porter's trolley along the platform.

'You wouldn't have enjoyed it,' he assured her. 'Tangier is a seedy tourist trap, as untypical of Morocco as Benidorm is of Spain.'

A guard in a smart brown uniform with a peaked cap was waiting at the entrance to the sleeping-car. He examined their tickets and led them along the corridor of the train till he came to Sarah's compartment. Opening the door, he ushered her inside.

The sleeper was a twin, there being no singles on the train. At present both bunks were folded away, the lower one behind the two armchairs with a small table between them. In a corner next to the window was a stainless steel wash-basin. A metal ladder to give access to the upper bunk was clipped to the wall.

While Sarah was glancing round her accommodation for the night, the porter came along the corridor and appeared in the doorway with her small case under his arm and the suitcase and hamper belonging to Carlos in his hands. He put all three pieces of luggage down on the floor of the compartment, and looked slightly surprised when Sarah thanked him and gave him the tip she had had ready in her pocket. Instead of picking up the suitcase and hamper, he left them where they were and started to leave, until Carlos pointed out that they didn't belong there. Then the guard intervened and a short conversation followed which Sarah couldn't understand, although when the guard began brandishing the tickets she began to have an inkling that something was amiss.

'It seems there's been a mistake . . . a double booking which the guard says can't be remedied because the train is crowded tonight. There are no empty sleepers,' Carlos explained to her.

'What! Oh, I can't believe it. How *could* they have made a mistake like that?'

'I don't know, but apparently they have. These things happen. We shall just have to make the best of it,' he said, with a philosophical shrug. 'It could be worse. It might have happened to strangers. At least we do know each other . . . and have in fact spent a night together quite recently,' he added, with a glint of amusement.

Sarah was *not* amused. 'Are you suggesting we should share?' she demanded incredulously.

'We have no choice,' said Carlos. 'If this chap'—with a glance at the guard—'had a spare compartment in reserve, he would already have intimated that, for a consideration, he might be able to find another berth somewhere. I think he's speaking the truth when he says the train is packed tonight. Which leaves us with the option of sharing or spending the night sitting up in an ordinary compartment with neighbours who may not have bathed recently, or who snore or have some other offensive habit. I don't propose to do that and I'm sure you don't wish to. You won't be disturbed by snores from me, by the way.'

'I know I shan't,' she retorted. 'Because you won't be sleeping in here. I made my booking before you and therefore I have first claim to this sleeper. I'm sorry if that leaves you to spend an uncomfortable night sandwiched between other passengers, but they may be perfectly clean, nice, respectable people. And you'll have the satisfaction of doing the gentlemanly thing,' she added sweetly.

'If this were a single sleeper, with only one bunk in it, of course I should do the gentlemanly thing and let you have it,' he agreed. 'But that isn't the situation. I have no intention of forgoing a decent night's sleep, lying down, merely because you don't like the idea of sharing. Be sensible, Sarah. I'm not suggesting we share a bunk. You'll be perfectly safe—I shan't lay a finger on you. While you're washing and changing, I'll stand outside in the corridor. It doesn't have to be an ordeal unless you choose to make it one.'

The way he put it, she did seem to be making a mountain out of a molehill. However, there was one aspect he had overlooked.

'It's not impossible there'll be someone on the train who knows you. I don't want to sound rude, but I can't pretend to like the idea of being taken for your latest girl-friend, which is the obvious implication if we're sharing a sleeper,' she pointed out.

The porter and guard decided to leave the two passengers to resolve the booking clerk's error as best they could. They had other passengers to attend to.

As they made to depart, Sarah said hurriedly, 'Don't let the porter go. You'll need him to move your luggage.' She would have stopped him herself, but her flustered brain refused to come up with the Spanish for, 'Wait! This gentleman's luggage needs to be moved elsewhere.'

Carlos made no attempt to detain the porter. He said, 'I can move the stuff myself . . . if necessary. I think the chances of either one of us seeing anyone we know is a small one, not worth worrying about.'

'Not worth your worrying about, perhaps. Your reputation is such that another snippet of scandal won't make any difference,' she declared hotly, angered by the guard's desertion.

She felt sure that, had a Spanish girl found herself in the same predicament, he would have supported her objections to sharing the sleeper. She remembered now seeing a hint of speculation in his eyes when she came on board with Carlos. Perhaps the guard thought that, being a blonde from one of the permissive countries in northern Europe, she wouldn't really mind sharing with a good-looking Spaniard and was protesting merely for form's sake.

'As bad as that, is it?' said Carlos, raising an eyebrow. 'I'm surprised your grandmother made no objection to your going to the *feria* with me. Perhaps she hasn't heard as many reports of my scandalous behaviour as you have.'

He spoke in a serious tone, with an expression to match, but she felt sure that inwardly he was laughing at her.

Then, with an abrupt change of subject, he said, 'You do realise there's no buffet car on this train?'

'Yes, I was warned. I brought some packed food with me.'

'So did I . . . and a bottle of wine. I hoped we should be having supper together, but perhaps you feel even that would do irreparable harm to your good name.' The remark, which could have been sarcastic if spoken with a cutting edge, was a gentle, good-humoured tease.

While Sarah searched for a reply, biting her lip in vexation at finding herself in this impossible situation, he went on, 'I tell you what: the most likely time for us to be seen together is now, while people are boarding.' He nodded in the direction of the window. It framed a view of the now bustling scene of activity on a platform from which, in less than half an hour's time, a long-distance train would set out on its night-long journey to Madrid at the heart of this vast, dry, mountainous country.

'So I'll disappear until the train starts and people have got themselves settled,' he continued. 'After which the only ones who might catch a glimpse of us eating together will be the people working on the land. I'll also have another word with the *jefe de tren*. It's possible there's someone else with a twin-berth sleeper——another man, I mean——who might be persuaded to let me share his compartment if the situation is explained to him.'

Without waiting for her reaction, he stepped into the corridor and closed the door, leaving her alone.

After fixing a worried frown on the door for a moment or two, Sarah made a conscious effort to compose herself. Lifting the hamper on to one of the chairs. She then moved his suitcase alongside the wall and swung her own lighter case on to a shelf above the door, leaving more room to move about in the already confined space. Then she sat down in the chair nearest the window and watched a trolley of mailbags being trundled past.

Now that she had time to consider the situation calmly and rationally, she realised how much more awkward it would have been if, as Carlos had remarked, her fellow victim of the clerk's inefficiency had been a man she had never set eyes on before.

She remembered how her heart had leapt when she had seen the Porsche in the street outside the station, and how pleasant it had been to be taken to the old-fashioned, dignified Octavio for coffee followed by a drink. As they had returned to the station, she had been looking forward to travelling with Carlos, even if not in the intimate circumstances which had been forced on them.

But was she really worried about someone seeing them together and jumping to a false conclusion? Was she really afraid that he would take advantage of the situation and pounce on her during the night?

The answer to both questions was No. At no time during their acquaintance had Carlos behaved unacceptably. In point of fact he had acted with the utmost chivalry. All she had against him, as it were, was Kristen's warning and her own instinctive feeling, at the beginning, that he *might* be a predatory male.

A priest in a black soutane and shallow-crowned

hat hurried past, followed by three youths in uniform, clearly recruits returning from or going on leave during their compulsory *mili* service. They were followed by a family of gypsies, not the colourful, free, footloose people of myth and romance, but a shifty-looking male followed by his heavily pregnant wife with an infant asleep on her shoulder and two grubby but well-fed children trailing behind.

Sarah's sympathies had always been easily engaged by underdogs and minority groups. But her attitude to Spanish gypsies had hardened since being begged for money by plump women with plump babies-in-arms who muttered unpleasantly when they weren't given alms and looked contemptuous when they were. She knew she wouldn't want to sit with the slatternly group who had gone past and, quite reasonably, neither would Carlos.

She made up her mind that, if there was no other unaccompanied man in the sleeping car who was prepared to share with him, she would accept the alternative with a good grace. The long stop-over in Madrid tomorrow would give them plenty of time to make sure they had separate accommodation on the second night of the journey.

The train had pulled out of the station and was slowly gathering speed through open undulating countryside still bathed in evening sunlight, when there was a knock on the door.

In case it wasn't Carlos outside, she called *'Adelante!'*

He came in and closed the door.

'I'm afraid the *jefe* hasn't been able to find another berth for me. I slipped him a tip to encourage his endeavours, but the only spare bunks are in a four-berth compartment whose occupants have only been married a few hours. Otherwise every berth is taken.'

'In that case we shall just have to make the best of it. Thinking it over I've realised it would be unfair to force you to spend the night in one of the ordinary coaches.' Sarah turned to look out of the window. 'I wish it stayed light here as long as it does in England at this time of year. There must be some marvellous scenery between here and Madrid, but we'll miss most of it in the dark.

Carlos removed the hamper from the other chair and sat down. 'Did you bring something to read? If not, I have several paperbacks and magazines. Shall we have another drink?'

He leaned forward to unstrap the hamper. It was equipped, Sarah saw, with silver, china plates, proper wine glasses and two bottles from which to fill them. The food was in plastic boxes and foil-wrapped parcels, and there seemed to be enough of it to feed several people.

'Your picnic is much grander than mine, but I do have a flask of coffee which you seem to lack,' she said.

He frowned. 'I hope not. Ah, here it is.' The vacuum flask had been hidden by the napkins. Not paper ones, linen.

'What's the joke?' he asked, when she laughed.

'I was thinking that if this sleeper had been occupied by an elderly maiden lady who adamantly refused to share it with you, you might have had to eat that feast Amparo prepared surrounded by a very scruffy gypsy family who are somewhere on the train,' she explained.

As expertly as a waiter, Carlos used a corkscrew on a bottle of white wine. 'Elderly ladies I can usually handle. Your grandmother liked me, I believe?'

'Yes, she did.'

'But you still have reservations? What makes you afraid to trust me? Trouble with another man?'

Sarah shook her head. 'I do trust you. I've agreed to share this compartment with you.'

He filled the glasses. 'How does your foot feel now? You're not limping at all, I notice.'

'It's almost completely back to normal, thanks to your good first aid.'

Carlos took the lid off a shallow container filled with black olives and placed it on the table between them. He picked up one of the glasses and raised it. *'Buen viaje, señorita.'*

'Buen viaje,' she echoed. Good journey.

Some hours later Sarah took off her dressing-gown and draped it across the foot of the lower bunk. Stepping out of her mules, she climbed between the crisp white cotton sheets. There was only one pillow. She turned it up on its end to cushion her shoulders while she read, and arranged the bedclothes to come high up under her armpits. Then she switched on her reading-light and put her watch on the small recessed shelf below it. Her final act before settling back with her book was to reach out and rap on the door, a signal to Carlos that he could come back in.

Although, when he did, she tried hard to concentrate on reading while he got ready for bed, the page might have been upside down for all the sense it made to her.

Without ever glancing at him, she was intensely aware of his activities at the basin. Stripped to the waist, as he had been the morning he had picked her up in his powerful arms, first he washed his face, neck and ears in the vigorous, splashy fashion which seemed to be universal among men and differed completely from a woman's way of washing herself. Next he brushed his teeth, taking some time over it. Finally he combed his hair.

Then, to her surprise and perhaps only because he was sharing the basin with her, he used a couple of tissues to wipe splashes off the mirror and leave everywhere neat.

Whether he looked at her as he hooked the ladder to his bunk and climbed up it, she didn't know. She kept her eyes on the text of her paperback.

Rattling and creaking its way through the Spanish night, the train was making too much noise for such slight sounds as the unfastening of a zip or the turning of a page to be audible from one bunk to the other. Carlos had switched off the overhead light and the one by the basin. It was the movements of his shadow, thrown by his reading-light on the opposite wall, that indicated he was changing his trousers for pyjama pants. Presently, neatly folded over the bar of a hanger, his trousers were suspended from the curtain rail.

Gradually, the strangeness of being in bed with a man who wasn't a brother, lover or close friend lying a few feet above her began to wear off. She found herself recovering her interest in the story she had begun the day before. The next time she glanced at her watch it was half past eleven, but people were still walking past in the corridor, speaking in normal voices, not expecting anyone to have turned out their lights at this—for Spain—early hour.

She must have nodded off. She woke, with a start, to find Carlos leaning over her.

'Don't be alarmed. I came down to put out your light. I leaned over to say goodnight and saw you had fallen asleep,' he said.

'Oh . . . you startled me. For a minute I couldn't think where I was.'

'Lie down and I'll tuck you up.' He was wearing dark blue silk pyjamas, the jacket unbuttoned to show his burnished brown chest.

Obediently she slid down the bed and he pulled the pillow into its normal position for her.

'Comfortable?'

'Yes, thank you. Goodnight, Carlos.'

'Goodnight.'

He reached across her to turn out the light. Briefly she felt the touch of his lips on her cheek. A moment later she saw him climbing the ladder. A few moments after that the upper berth light was extinguished. The compartment was in darkness.

Touching the place he had kissed with the tips of her fingers, Sarah gave a happy little sigh and went back to sleep.

On advice given to her grandmother by someone who had done the journey, it had been Sarah's intention, on arrival at Madrid's Chamartín station, to put her case and her tote bag in a coin-operated locker. Carlos had other ideas.

A porter was instructed to take their luggage to a taxi. Sarah didn't catch the address Carlos gave to the driver, but as the cab moved off he turned to her and said, 'I always book a day-room in Madrid when I use the motorail. As you've already been hopelessly compromised, it would be foolish to object to having a bath or a shower, whichever you prefer, in the room which is at my disposal.'

The room turned out to be a suite at the Ritz Hotel where he was greeted by some of the older members of staff with a warmth reserved for someone they had known since he was a small boy. To Sarah's relief there was none of the prurient surmise she had detected in the eyes of the guard on the train in these people's attitude. She might have been Carlos's wife or his sister. Whatever they were thinking, there was nothing in their manner to suggest that there was anything irregular in Don Carlos, as they called him, being accompanied by a young woman.

In any case, overnight her feelings towards him, herself and the world in general had changed. When she had opened her eyes this morning, the curtains had been drawn back, the sun had been shining in and Carlos had been shaving at the basin. In one of life's moments of truth, she had known she was no longer in danger of loving him. She *did* love him. She ought to have known it the day before, when the thought of never seeing him again had made the future look bleak until the sight of his car had filled her with joy.

She had first use of the bathroom while he made some telephone calls.

'I have various elderly relations here who will be offended if I don't at least say hello on my way through,' he explained. 'Is there anything you want pressed while you're having your bath?'

Earlier, after washing and putting on her make-up while once more he stood in the corridor. Sarah had changed the trousers and shirt in which she had started the journey for a full, swingy skirt and matching cotton top.

'Is this smart enough for Madrid?' she asked.

His dark eyes swept her from head to foot. 'You look exactly right for the time of year. In winter this city is like the retreat from Moscow, in summer like the Equator. But in late spring and autumn the climate is perfect.'

The hotel provided a white bathrobe, a cap, the finest quality soap or shower gel. It was an unexpected treat to stretch out in a tub of warm water at this stage of the journey. She remembered she had promised to call her grandmother and would do so while Carlos was showering. But she didn't think she would mention where she was or who she was with. Time enough for that later, when she knew her feelings were reciprocated. Suddenly it seemed very possible that this wonderful man was beginning to feel the way she did. He had changed his plans to travel back with her. He had kissed her goodnight very gently and tenderly. Surely, surely it had to mean that he was beginning to care for her in a special way?

When Carlos emerged from the bathroom, his black hair damp from the shower, she had opened one of the balconied windows in the sitting-room and was admiring the view over the trees of the Plaza de la Lealtad which lay just off the teeming main thoroughfare which had brought them from the railway station to the heart of the city.

'What is that obelisk?' she asked, looking at a tall monument rising from among the trees.

Carlos came to stand beside her. 'It commemorates the heroes of May the second, 1808; the leaders of the Spanish uprising against Napoleon. There's a famous painting by Goya called *Fusilamientos,* which means executions by firing squad, in the Prado Museum. I thought we'd go to the Prado some time today. It's just round the corner.'

At this point their breakfast arrived, wheeled in by a waiter in a tail-coat and a wing collar and black bow tie. There was a bottle of champagne on the trolley, Sarah noticed, remembering their previous breakfast together and Carlos telling her

he always had champagne on Sundays, special days
and after nights without sleep. Today must qualify
as a special day. Perhaps—oh, let it be true!—he
had looked at her lying in her bunk, when she said
good morning to him, and realised he was in love
with her.

'Is there anything you particularly want to see, or
will you rely on me to show you the city?' he asked,
while they were eating at a table set before the open
window.

She explained about the presents for her father
and Harriet which she hadn't been able to buy in
Algeciras yesterday. 'I should like to take something
back for them, if there's time for a little shopping.'

'Plenty of time. You can help me choose a present
for Elizabeth . . . my secretary. The train doesn't
leave until twenty to eight this evening. We have
ample time to shop, see some of the sights and have
a leisurely lunch. There's a restaurant car on tonight's
train, but I'm doubtful whether it serves anything
worth eating, so I'm getting the hotel to refill the
hamper for another picnic. I hope that's all right
with you?'

She nodded. 'Fine.'

It had not been necessary to remind him, before
leaving the station, that their separate reservations
on the Paris train needed confirming. Tonight they
would have a choice of compartments in which to
eat whatever the Ritz provided for them. Secretly,
she was a little sorry there *was* space for them to
sleep apart. Once or twice during last night the train
had hurtled over the points with a noise and a
movement which had woken and slightly alarmed
her. It had been comforting to know that Carlos
was there; that in any kind of emergency, minor or
major, he would take care of her.

'My Spanish grandfather stayed here soon after the hotel opened almost ninety years ago . . . perhaps in this suite,' said Carlos, pouring some more coffee for her. 'The hotel was built at the command of King Alfonso III, the present King's grandfather. He'd been on a world tour and realised that what Madrid lacked was a great hotel. Who better to master-mind it than César Ritz who'd already built the Paris Ritz and the London Ritz.'

'I've never been in a really grand hotel before,' she said. 'Do they always have such fabulous carpets?'

She had noticed that the thick gold carpet in the bedroom had a border of flowers which exactly enclosed the twin beds and here in the sitting-room the carpet's design followed the curve of the outside wall. Downstairs and in the corridors, all the flowers were covered with similarly deep-piled, elaborate carpets.

'Usually, but the carpets here were all handmade at the Royal Tapestry Factory. As carpets go, they're considered masterpieces,' Carlos answered. 'I'm told the hotel employs two women who do nothing else but go round repairing any worn patches.'

What must it cost, Sarah wondered, to stay amid all this opulence? There were cut flowers in the bedroom, and the gilded Louis Quinze writing table was generously supplied with tissue-lined envelopes and die-stamped writing paper.

When, later, they left the hotel, the doorman would have summoned a taxi, but Carlos suggested walking to stretch their legs.

They went first to the Puerta del Sol—the Gateway of the Sun—which he told her was Madrid's equivalent of Piccadilly Circus in London.

'If you like we can look round two major department stores, El Corte Inglés and Galerias Preciados, which are near here,' he said, 'but I think you'll find their merchandise very similar to John Lewis's or Selfridges's. The smaller shops have more unusual things.'

And higher prices, no doubt, was Sarah's thought. However, she found that even in the rather exclusive atmosphere of the shop where he went to buy a bag for his secretary, the prices were substantially below those of fine leather goods in England.

Although he had said she could help him make a choice, in fact Carlos needed no advice either from her or the English-speaking assistant, with whom he conversed in that language so that Sarah could follow what was being said.

'I'm looking for a summer bag for a woman of middle age who always wears plain tailored clothes,' he explained. 'Not too small and not white.

Several bags were produced from which he selected a classic shoulder bag of beautiful bone-coloured calf, lined with suede and fitted with several zipped pockets.

'What do you think?' he asked Sarah.

'I think she's a very lucky secretary.'

'She's my right hand,' he answered. 'A more sensible, efficient, conscientious woman it would be impossible to find. I'm lucky to have her.'

Sarah brought a less expensive but very nice bag for Harriet, two bill-folds to put by for her brothers' birthdays and, as an extra present for him, a leather belt for her father.

'What about you? Nothing for you?' asked Carlos.

'If it wouldn't be a terrible bore for you, I'd like to buy myself some shoes.'

He glanced downwards. 'With those legs, how could it be boring?'

She laughed. 'I promise not to take long about it.'

Luckily, at the first shop she tried they had what she wanted in her size; a pair of high-heeled leather sandals, the same colour as her sun-tanned legs, to wear with all her summer dresses on occasions which called for something more elegant than espadrilles.

With Carlos insisting on carrying all the parcels, they then strolled up to the Plaza Mayor, for long the hub of the city and once the scene of the bullfights, the canonisations of saints and the terrible public punishments of the Spanish Inquisition.

Now the great square with its nine arched gateways and ornate façades above arcaded walks had an open-air café where they had mid-morning coffee.

'On Sunday mornings there's a stamp and coins market here, or alternatively there's the Rastro, the flea-market,' Carlos told her. 'One needs at least a week to see Madrid properly. It's a pity we have to leave for the station before the night life begins. I don't mean the theatres and floor-shows but the street life. People dine late here, not before ten or eleven. Afterwards they sit in the cafés and bars or go for a walk. In this part of the city, the streets are still full of people at two or three in the morning.' He looked at her intently. 'Perhaps we can join them another time.'

'I hope so,' she answered. In case she had read a meaning into the last remark which he hadn't intended, she played safe by adding, 'Spain is a fascinating country . . . quite different from the rest of Europe.'

'Some people think it really belongs to Africa. Certainly the long Moorish occupation had a permanent influence on our looks and our ways.'

The hot bright sunlight burned down on his thick

black hair and the bronzed skin stretched tautly across the high slant of his cheekbones. Sarah wondered if, centuries ago, one of the Moslem conquerors had taken a Spanish girl into his harem, bequeathing to all their descendants his dark eyes—and perhaps also his attitude to women.

They had been fierce, ruthless men, those long-ago invaders; riding their agile Arab horses with razor-sharp stirrups to slash the Spanish horses' tendons. But in other ways they had been civilised, introducing science, culture and beautiful buildings and gardens to a barbarous land.

Having seen Carlos on the polo field, it was easy to imagine him, in another age, riding fearlessly into battle, or leaning from his saddle to scoop up a girl who had taken his fancy, carrying her off to become at first his plaything but then perhaps, later on, the loved and cherished mother of his sons.

'You've gone away somewhere,' he said, leaning towards her.

Caught out in a romantic fantasy in which she had been the girl he wanted—thank goodness he couldn't read her mind!—she said, 'Only into Spain's past.'

From the café in the Plaza Mayor, they walked a short way to the gardens of another *plaza* in front of the enormous Palacio Real, the palace of Spain's Bourbon kings.

'I wanted you to see this,' said Carlos, leading her up to a larger than life-size bronze sculpture of a man astride a prancing horse. 'The rider is Philip the Fourth. I think it's the finest equestrian statue in Europe. It was designed by Velásquez who, in Spain, is considered the world's greatest artist. The actual sculptor was a Florentine, Tacca.'

Sarah had never heard of Tacca and even Velásquez was only a famous name to her. It crossed her mind that as soon as she had the chance she had better take a crash course in art appreciation before Carlos discovered her almost total ignorance on a subject which, clearly, was important to him. She hoped it would interest her more when she knew something about it.

They spent an hour inside the palace, but it was too vast and filled with too many treasures for everything to be seen in a single visit.

'I don't want to give you cultural indigestion,' he said, smiling down at her, as they came out into the sunshine.

She wondered if he suspected that her interest had been beginning to flag. She hoped not. She knew that to sustain the love of a man like Carlos, a woman would have to keep him interested intellectually as well as physically. It would be fatal to bore him.

They returned to the streets of shops and bars where he took her to one which was famous for its selection of delicious *tapas* to be eaten with a small glass of wine to stimulate the appetite for a late lunch.

She had eaten *tapas* before, but never from a range as diverse and tempting as the dishes set out on the long counter of a bar in a back street too narrow to admit vehicles and not one tourists would find except by accident. Sarah was the only foreigner there, and the only woman. All the other customers were well-groomed men, not wearing dark grey or navy as they would in a bar in the City of London, but dressed in summer-weight suits in beige and other light colours appropriate to the heat in the streets. They glanced at her and Carlos, who was casually clad in a dark red cotton-knit shirt and palest grey linen trousers, his folded sun-glasses hooked in the opening of his shirt.

The *tapas* were both hot and cold; the hot ones being fried in pans of sizzling olive oil on hobs behind the bar, or cooked *a la plancha* on a heated slab, rather than being re-heated in the micro-wave ovens of the tourist resorts.

Sitting on a tall stool, Sarah sampled *pinchitos* of veal speared on sticks, small prawns, mussels in scarlet *pimiento* sauce, slivers of spicy sausage and crispy little whitebait, all accompanied by crusty fresh bread.

'Do we *need* lunch after that?' she asked laughingly, when they left the bar.

'By half past two you'll be hungry again. Meanwhile we're going to jump into a taxi, drop these parcels at the hotel and go for a stroll in the Retiro.'

The Retiro turned out to be a very large park with shady walks and a boating lake. After the noise and the fumes of traffic in the streets and the heat of the pavements at noon, it was pleasant to wander on grass with the sounds of the city reduced to a hum in the background of the birdsong.

As they walked and talked, it was Carlos who did most of the talking while Sarah listened and asked questions. She couldn't help wishing she had had a more interesting life and therefore more to contribute to the conversation. But of course he was older and widely travelled. It was inevitable that he could discuss a wider range of subjects and experiences.

Suddenly he took her hand, making her glance upwards to meet a look in his eyes which made her catch her breath. Her fingers trembled in the light clasp of his. All at once the inside of her throat felt

dry and constricted, but not the way that it did at
the start of a cold.

Carlos came to a halt. He glanced round. There
was no one within two hundred yards of them. He
slipped his other arm around her and drew her
towards him. Slowly, he bent his head, touching his
mouth lightly to hers, moving his lips very softly
and gently at first and then with increasing insistence
until, like spontaneous combustion, something
ignited and they were locked together, his arms
crushing her to him, her arms flung round his neck.

It was a long kiss and it left Sarah limp and
breathless, shaken by the most overwhelming wave
of feeling she had ever known.

She rested her cheek against his shoulder and
heard him say huskily, 'I've wanted to do that since
the first night when you wouldn't stay and talk to
me *à deux*.'

'I was afraid, if I did, you *would* do it,' she
admitted.

'Why afraid?'

'It was too soon. I didn't know you.'

He turned her face up to his. 'But you wanted me
to kiss you. Admit it.'

'I do.'

He smiled. 'Was it worth waiting for?'

She found it impossible to dissemble. 'Yes . . .
you know it was.'

'For me, too,' he said, gazing deeply into her eyes.
'It's not my nature to be patient, but perhaps it is
true that the best things are worth waiting for.'

'Oh, Carlos . . . ' The words *I love you* trembled
on her tongue. She only just managed to check
them; wanting him to say them first, although every
instinct told her he felt exactly as she did—that the

world was no longer the same place as it had been before they kissed.

He would have kissed her again, but now there were people aproaching. Reluctantly, he drew away and, keeping hold of her hand, resumed their walk.

'This place is far too public. I didn't choose my moment well . . . but I couldn't put it off any longer. I had to feel you in my arms,' he said, a few moments later.

Sarah thought of the suite at the Ritz and wondered if, after lunch, he would want to return there instead of going to the Prado to look at paintings.

Siesta. A word widely known outside Spain where it had two meanings. The hottest part of the day, the afternoon heat and also a nap or sleep . . . or a time to make love. The thought of a *siesta* with Carlos made her pulses race. At the same time she wasn't sure it was what she really wanted . . . not yet . . . not today.

Like their first kiss, surely their first *siesta* would be worth waiting for? They had only just begun to reveal their hearts to each other. Couldn't they spin it out . . . savour each sweet discovery before going on to the next? That was the way she would like it. But as he had already said, it wasn't his way to be patient; and if he wanted her, how could she refuse him?

'Now for the second most famous woman in European painting,' said Carlos, a few paces before they came to one of the Prado Museum's great treasures, Goya's *La Maja Desnuda:* a full-length portrait of a black-eyed beauty reclining, naked, on cushions, her right arm behind her head.

'What does *maja* mean?' Sarah asked.

'It means a working-class woman, especially a *madrileña,* a woman of this city. But in fact she was an aristocrat . . . the Duchess of Alba.'

'She and Goya were lovers, presumably?' Sarah was drawing that conclusion from the subject's relaxed and uninhibited pose and the expression in her eyes as she watched—not, as she seemed to, the people passing through the gallery—the artist who, long ago, had immortalised her lovely body. Although there was something rather odd about her bosom. It seemed unnaturally buoyant, more like two balloons than breasts.

'Presumably,' Carlos agreed, his eyes on the *maja's* shapely legs.

Sarah decided to keep her criticism to herself. The Goya was the last of about a dozen pictures he had selected as the cream of the Prado's masterpieces. 'Although not all the professional art critics would agree with my choice,' he had told her, when they arrived at the museum after lunching in a restaurant which had been catering to Spanish gourmets for almost two centuries.

The unaccustomed hour—Mrs Grantham still lunched at one—and Sarah's emotional state had combined to prevent her from doing full justice to the asparagus mousse followed by crayfish *ensalada* with watercress which she had chosen as two of the lighter specialities of the house. It had been impossible to concentrate on food so soon after Carlos had kissed her for the first time. She had felt in a happy daze, shot through with some apprehension about his plans for the remainder of the afternoon.

The heat of noonday had abated when they left the Prado and walked past the fountains playing in the Plaza Cánovas to the nearby Ritz.

On the way, Carlos looked at his watch. 'There's just time to have tea and a shower before we leave for the station.'

They had tea under a vine-shaded pergola in the hotel's garden, sitting on a blue-cushioned white wicker sofa while another tail-coated waiter laid a tea table for them.

Later, Carlos gave Sarah the key to the suite and sent her upstairs to shower while he read *El Pais,* one of Spain's daily newspapers.

This time she took off her make-up and used a sachet of shampoo provided by the hotel to wash the dust of the city out of her hair.

Standing under the cascade of water, shampoo-suds sliding down her body as she rinsed and re-rinsed her mop of curls before using her own favourite conditioner, she wondered if it might be the Spanish side of Carlos which had restrained him from rushing her into bed when he had had the opportunity.

She had seen for herself that manners were more formal here. Even teenagers shook hands and performed the ritual of kissing each other on both cheeks when they met. Probably other codes of behaviour were also stricter. If, for the first time in his life, Carlos was serious, it might be that he felt he ought to present himself to her family before making more than the lightest love to her.

But before she could take him home with her and introduce him to her father, she had to break it off with Jamie, she remembered, with a frown. It was an awkward situation, being ecstatically in love with Carlos while everyone who knew her—including Jamie himself—assumed she was as good as engaged to young Dr Drayton. They were not to know, even people close to her didn't, that the break with Jamie had been brewing for a long time.

She was dressed and had almost finished blow-drying her hair when Carlos tapped on the bedroom door.

'Come in.' She switched off her dryer and laid it down on the dressing-table where she was sitting.

He didn't go straight to the bathroom but came to stand behind the dressing-stool, smiling at her through the mirror.

'You've washed your hair, I see.'

'I wash it most days, but didn't expect to have the chance today. If I'd been travelling alone, I should now be going back to the station all hot and sticky instead of completely refreshed.'

'You've never looked anything but cool and lovely,' he told her. He put his hands on her shoulders and bent to kiss the top of her head. 'Mm . . . it smells good . . . and feels like silk.' He twisted a curl round his finger. His other hand moved to her neck, loosely half-circling the base of her throat, his thumb gently rubbing her nape.

Even that light caress sent shivers of delight through her. Also a pang of regret that the beds reflected in the mirror were still neatly covered, unused. She was his for as long as she lived; committed in heart and mind. Why withhold the rest of herself? Now she wished he *had* brought her back here instead of going to the Prado to look at the portrait of a woman who had not only known love's raptures but been painted in their languorous aftermath.

'I'd better get under the shower,' said Carlos.

He disappeared, leaving her to wonder if the remark had had a double meaning; not only that it would soon be time for them to leave, but that touching her had kindled a heat in his blood which a cold shower would douse.

She had put on fresh make-up and re-packed her toilet bag when he joined her in the sitting-room, his red shirt changed for one of terracotta linen. Both colours suited his Mediterranean colouring.

A tap on the door heralded the arrival of a baggage porter to take their cases down.

Carlos must have dealt with the bill before he came upstairs, as he didn't head for the desk when they left the lift. They crossed the marbled entrance hall, passed under a half-moon fanlight with the hotel's double *R* monogram silhouetted against the light, and stepped into a waiting taxi. The doorman folded one gloved palm over some notes and touched his peaked cap with the other, and the taxi glided forward. Soon they were passing Cibeles, the most famous of all the city's fountains. The day in Madrid was over, every hour of it unforgettable, but especially the moment in the park when they had embraced.

As if he were thinking the same thing, Carlos reached for Sarah's hand and held it all the way back to Chamartín.

They had their picnic supper in his compartment. For the second time that day they drank champagne. As well as filling the hamper with ambrosial things from the chef's cold buffet, the hotel had provided a bottle of vintage champagne, another of white wine and a third of spring water, all packed in a coolbox. The casual extravagance of Carlos's habits took Sarah's breath away, used as she was to the economies and inconveniences of ordinary people's lives.

Again, to her disappointment, night had fallen before she had seen as much of the central sierras as she would have liked. The train's route to France was by way of Burgos and Irún, crossing the Spanish border about two in the morning and arriving in Paris shortly before nine tomorrow.

'Years ago, people had to change trains at the border,' Carlos told her. 'Spanish railway tracks are wider than French ones. But now the Talgo not only has a suspension system which allows it to take curves faster than other trains, but also displaceable wheels which can travel on both widths of track with only a short reduction of speed where they merge.'

They had left the curtains undrawn. From time to time, as they ate, the lights of a village or an isolated farmhouse in the mountains showed in the darkness outside.

'How long would this journey have taken in the days of horse and carriage travel?' Sarah mused aloud. 'Weeks and weeks, I suppose. Even by car, on today's roads, it would be a long gruelling run.'

'What time are your family expecting you home tomorrow?'

'I said I'd telephone from Dover to let them know I'd arrived safely. I had thought I might stay with a friend in Kent tomorrow night. It all depends which cross-Channel ferry I catch. I haven't booked a passage. Have you?'

He shook his head. 'It isn't necessary outside the school holiday periods. If you don't have to get back on any specific day, how about spending tomorrow with me in Paris?'

She didn't hesitate. 'I'd love to!'

'I know a good small hotel in a little place called Ardres, near Calais. If we leave Paris in time to avoid the rush hour, we can get there in time for dinner tomorrow night. Then we can make an early crossing the following morning and arrive at your home by mid-afternoon.

The last part of the plan was unexpected; she had thought she would have at the very least a few hours' grace before he presented himself on her father's doorstep.

'But shouldn't you go to London?' she asked. 'I'd have thought, after being away, you would have a mass of things waiting for your attention.'

'I doubt it . . . and having escorted you this far, I'd like to see you safely to your door. I'm sure you're perfectly competent to change a wheel, or deal with any contingency which might arise, but I'd rather do it for you.'

Jamie had never made her feel cherished like this. Even when he was beginning to love her, he had never behaved as if it would be his mission in life to shield her from every discomfort and annoyance. The son of a woman who had selflessly devoted herself to the care of her 'menfolk' as she called them—in a tone which implied they were higher beings—he would expect Sarah to be like his mother.

Although Carlos had lost both his parents when he was eight, she sensed from his references to her that his mother had left him a memory of a beautiful woman, adoring and adored by her husband. Sarah felt that what Carlos needed was not to be looked after—other people could do that for him—but to be loved in the way Cristina Velada had loved Charles Hastings, leaving her country for him and letting him risk his neck on the Cresta Run because it was what he enjoyed.

'Would you rather I didn't come home with you?' Carlos asked.

'No . . . but it might disconcert my stepmother. She's one of those people who like plenty of warning.'

'Telephone her from Ardres tomorrow night. That should be enough warning.'

'Yes . . . yes, I expect so.' Suppressing her misgivings, she asked, 'Do you know Paris as well as you know Madrid?'

Because they had lunched late, they had also eaten their supper later than the night before. It was about half past eleven when Sarah got up to go.

'Thank you for a lovely day, Carlos. I shouldn't have enjoyed it half as much on my own . . . or seen all the things you showed me.'

He had risen with her. 'It was a pleasure for me.' He took her face in his hands. 'Must you go? Must you leave me?'

As it had in the park some hours earlier, her breath seemed to catch in her throat. Her cheeks, already pink from the wine, flushed a deeper rose under the golden brown of her Sotogrande tan.

'I—I think I must,' she murmured.

His thumb brushed across her warm cheeks to touch the corners of her mouth. 'I should very much like you to stay.' He spoke in a deep quiet voice which made her weak at the knees.

'Oh, Carlos . . . ' she whispered helplessly, feeling her will-power slipping away.

'Kiss me goodnight.' He said the last word with his mouth to her temple.

She closed her eyes, feeling his warm lips slide softly down her cheek, seeking her half-parted lips. Like their first kiss in the Retiro, it began gently but almost at once grew fiercer. His arms tightened round her. His mouth became more demanding.

Dimly, in a corner of her mind, like a candle flame exposed to a draught, there was a flickering doubt that she was behaving wisely in yielding to the delight of feeling the breadth of his shoulders under her exploring palms, of being pressed to his powerful male body.

Then the emotions aroused by his insistent lips, his caressing hands, extinguished all rational thought, leaving her at the mercy of her clamorous senses.

CHAPTER FIVE

THE train glided slowly into the Gare d'Austerlitz. As soon as it stopped, doors swung open and passengers swarmed on to the platform, hurrying in search of luggage carts, summoning porters, or carrying their baggage in the direction of the shuttle-bus service which would take them to the nearby motorail yard where their cars would be unloaded.

As Carlos stepped out of the door at the end of the corridor and turned to give his hand to Sarah, an announcement came over the public address system. It sounded less adenoidal than most British station announcements and it wasn't necessary for Carlos to translate it for her. Her French was equal to the message, which was: *Would Monsieur Carlos 'Astings, a passenger on the train from Madrid, please go to Information where an urgent message awaits him.* It was then repeated. *Would Monsieur Carlos 'Astings . . .*

'Oh dear . . . I hope it's not bad news,' she said anxiously, as the porter followed her out of the train with their luggage.

Carlos shrugged. 'Probably a minor crisis which won't take long to deal with.' He had kept hold of her hand. As they began to walk down the platform, he lifted it to his lips and brushed a kiss across her knuckles. 'Don't worry: I won't allow anything to interfere with our day in Paris.'

But after calling the number given him at the

station's Information desk, he had to retract that
assurance.

'I'm afraid this a major crisis. My uncle has had
a heart attack in America. His condition is critical
and my aunt needs me there. If I leave here
immediately, I can catch the French Concorde and
be in New York in a few hours. There isn't even
time to wait for my car to be unloaded—I'll go to
the airport by taxi. I'm sorry, but I've got to desert
you.'

'I understand. Of course you must go at once.
Don't worry about me, but what about your car?'

'Someone on our French staff will see to it. I'll
call you tonight. Goodbye.' Regardless of the
watching porter, and all the other people around
them, he took her in his arms and kissed her hard
on the mouth.

Then grabbing his case from the trolley, he turned
away.

'But you haven't got my number——' she began.

It was too late. He didn't hear her. His mind on
catching the flight which would take him to his
uncle's bedside, he was dodging his way through the
crowd in what he must know was the direction of
the taxi rank.

Anyway, not knowing someone's telephone
number wouldn't prevent a man like Carlos from
making contact, she thought with a faint smile, the
feel of that swift possessive kiss still on her lips.

The Lancia had yet to be unloaded when Sarah
arrived at the motorail depot. It was a peculiarity of
her grandfather's car that it needed several pumps
on the accelerator to make it start easily. The
unloader hadn't known this, and when it came off
the transporter the battery was flat. However, the
depot had a portable battery charger and the delay

wasn't a long one. Soon Sarah was behind the wheel, keeping a sharp look-out for directional signs and rather wishing there was a silver Porsche ahead of her to lead the way to the north side of Paris and the autoroute to Calais. After more than thirty-six hours of Carlo's protective pampering, she couldn't help feeling slightly bereft now that she was no longer under his wing.

Driving round the Boulevard Périphérique, the crowded eight-lane road encircling Paris and linking the many motorways which converged on the city, was not an experience she enjoyed in a car which still felt unfamiliar. But the slip-roads were clearly marked and it wasn't long before she was on the A1 with a pleasant run through northern France on a sunny day ahead of her.

Signs for Charles de Gaulle airport indicated that this was the road Carlos had travelled in a taxi about an hour earlier. When the autoroute swept through a tunnel under the airport's runaways, Sarah wondered if he was already airborne in the amazing aircraft which crossed the Atlantic in three and a half hours from London and presumably not much longer from Paris.

From what he had told her, there wasn't much love lost between him and the uncle who had taken charge of his upbringing after his parents were killed; but he was very fond of his aunt and it would be to support and comfort her that he was rushing to New York.

Kristen had made him out to be a man of predatory habits and few scruples where women were concerned, and perhaps he had been in the past, with women attracted to him for reasons other than his personal qualities. But now that she knew him, Sarah felt sure that with any woman he cared for or valued—his aunt, his young Spanish kinswoman Isabel, his secretary or herself—he would always be kind and considerate to a degree.

Near the historic town of Arras, the autoroute split, one way heading for Lille and the border with Belguim and the other turning west towards the coast of Normandy and the ferry ports.

Sarah arrived at Calais in time to join a line of cars about to drive on to a hovercraft. She knew the crossing by hovercraft wasn't as enjoyable as by ship, but it was much quicker, and she had changed her mind about spending the night in Kent. She wanted to get home as fast as possible to be there when Carlos rang up.

Sitting in the hovercraft cabin, unable to see very much through the spray on the windows, and disliking the noise and vibration, she thought of Carlos who, if Concorde had taken off shortly after he reached the airport, should touch down in America at about the same time the hovercraft subsided on the landing pad at Dover.

By now their long journey together had begun to seem vaguely unreal. She could almost believe that at any moment she would wake up to find herself lying on a sun-bed by the pool at Sotogrande, having dreamt the whole thing except for the very beginning of it; seeing a tall attractive man at Málaga airport who, shortly afterwards, had looked right through her.

However, when she was waved to a halt, going through the green lane of the Customs at Dover, and asked to open her tailgate, the picnic hamper was tangible proof that last night and the night before, and the day in Madrid, had not been a dream, or wishful thinking, but a real and wonderful experience.

Perhaps because a young sun-tanned girl driving a sporty-looking car seemed a likely smuggler, or perhaps for the simple reason that he was also in his twenties and not many of the people he searched radiated the joy of living, the Customs officer didn't hurry his inspection.

Before she left the docks area, Sarah had a short telephone conversation with Harriet who said, in her blighting way, that the weather had been atrocious and they were recovering from bad colds.

'Welcome home! Can't wait to see you,' Sarah murmured wryly to herself, as she replaced the receiver.

But as it wasn't Harriet's nature to be delighted to see anyone, she knew it was foolish to have hoped for a more enthusiastic reaction to her return.

Driving from Dover to London, she rehearsed ways of telling Jamie she could never be his wife. In that respect, the message summoning Carlos to New York had been a godsend, giving her time to to straighten out her past before embarking on her future.

Thinking it over, she was inclined to believe that it would be Jamie's pride rather than his heart which would be most injured by being, in effect, jilted.

If it hadn't been for subtle pressure from his mother, would he ever have looked at the girl next door, so to speak, except in a brotherly way? Sarah remembered from several years ago when the then Lady Diana Spencer had been front page news, she had been described as 'the Clarence House candidate', meaning the Queen Mother had hoped she would be the girl Prince Charles would choose for his bride. She knew she had been Dr and Mrs Drayton's candidate. They had been aware of her schoolgirl crush on their son and had seen it outlast her teens. Dr Drayton had delivered Sarah and always been fond of her. His wife, known in the village as a good, kind woman but also something of a snob, had no doubt liked the idea of her son marrying Colonel Lancaster's daughter. Undoubtedly she had been instrumental in making Jamie take notice of Sarah in a way which, for long, he had not.

In her lukewarm way, Harriet Lancaster seemed pleased with the bag Sarah had chosen for her, and her father was delighted with the cigars, a luxury he rarely allowed himself being, like all owners of old houses, forever worried by the ever-rising cost of repairs.

'I'll have one after dinner tonight,' he said, having thanked his daughter warmly for her present.

'I've invited Jamie to join us,' said Harriet. 'He's been very down in the mouth while you've been away, his mother says. He was expecting a letter from you . . . not just postcards,' she added, on a note of reproach.

In other words Celia Drayton feels I should have written a letter, thought Sarah, masking her irritation. At one time she had been glad of Mrs Drayton's close interest in her son's life, being equally interested herself and liking to go round and listen to his mother talking about him. Since then, she had realised that to live in the same village as one's mother-in-law and be under her constant surveillance would be extremely trying, especially as Mrs Drayton was a model housewife and would expect Sarah to live up to her exacting standards.

Jamie was late arriving and the Lancasters were having the ritual glass of dry sherry in the shabby but pleasant drawing-room when they heard his car crunching over the gravel.

'Aren't you going to let him in?' said Harriet, when her stepdaughter didn't jump up and rush to meet him.

'He knows where to find us,' said Sarah, who wanted to avoid an embrace in the hall.

A few moments later Jamie burst in, full of apologies and explanations for his lateness. After greeting his host and hostess, he turned to Sarah, kissing her cheek before saying, 'That's a fabulous tan. How was the trip back? No problems?'

'No problems at all. How are you? Have you managed to dodge this 'flu-cold Harriet says everyone's had?'

'Yes, thank goodness. It wouldn't have done for Dad and me to be under the weather this past fortnight. It's been all go since you left.' He began to relate the illnesses and accidents which had happened during her absence.

Listening to him and to the comments of her father and Harriet, she realised that, now she was safely back, none of them was the slightest bit interested in what she had seen and done on her trip abroad. To all three, the place where they lived was the centre of the universe and the butcher's wife's gallstones and old Mr Rowburn's bad fall were of far greater moment than how Molly Grantham was getting on or what Sarah had thought of Madrid and seen on her fourteen-hundred-mile journey from the Straits of Gibraltar to the English Channel.

Perhaps she noticed their parochialism more after being in the company of a man with a cosmopolitan outlook. She glanced at her watch, wondering what time he would ring up.

The call came when she was in the kitchen helping Harriet to dish up. The telephone was in the hall with one extension in her father's bedroom. When she hurried into the hall, Colonel Lancaster had already picked up the receiver.

'Hello?'

Sarah was close enough to hear a woman's voice with an American accent say, 'I have a call from New York for Miss Sarah Lancaster. Is Miss Lancaster there, please?'

'She is. I'll put her on.' Looking puzzled, her father handed over the telephone.

'Sarah Lancaster speaking.' Her heart had begun to race. She wished her father would hurry back to the drawing-room and shut the door.

'I have Mr Hastings for you. One moment, please.' There was a short pause and then, as clearly as if it were a local call, she heart the unmistakable voice of her love saying, 'You're safely back at home. That's good. I'm sorry I had to desert you so abruptly.

'It doesn't matter. How is your uncle?'

'Still hanging on, but his chances aren't good.'

'And your aunt? How is she?'

'She was very distressed when I got here. There had been no warning . . . no previous heart trouble. Any bad shock is harder in unfamiliar surroundings, among strangers, however helpful.'

'I can imagine. It was lucky you could get there quickly.'

'My cousins are coming over on the late Concorde flight. They'll be here this evening. She'll have us all with her if my uncle dies. How was the Channel crossing? Smooth, I imagine?'

'Like glass. The only two minor hitches were a flat battery at the depot—but they soon put that right—and being searched by the Customs at Dover. Otherwise it all went swimmingly. Having survived the Boulevard Périphérique, with French drivers changing lanes in every direction, and juggernauts thundering on all sides, I feel I could drive anywhere!'

'If things had gone according to plan, we should now be having aperitifs at the Hotel Clément at Ardres. Are you missing me?'

'Yes . . . very much.'

'There are things I want to say to you, but not on the telephone. I don't know when I shall be able to get back. It depends what happens here.'

'Of course . . . I understand that. By the way, I have your hamper here. Afterwards I realised I should have put it in the boot of your car, but——'

'It isn't important. Don't worry about it.'

Having completed her tasks in the kitchen, Harriet came through the hall, pausing to signal to Sarah that she should conclude her conversation because Harriet was about to summon the men to the dining-room where the first course was already set out. It would not occur to her, and indeed why should it in the circumstances, that this call might be more important than sitting down, on time, to eat a slice of somewhat under-ripe, ungarnished melon.

Sarah said, speaking to Carlos, 'We'll be having dinner soon and then I'll have an early night. If you're five hours behind, you're going to be exhausted by the time you go to bed.'

'I slept for most of the flight. There was no one sitting next to me and I asked not to be disturbed. I can manage on very little sleep when I have to.'

The men were emerging from the drawing-room and following Harriet across the hall to the dining-room. Longing for privacy, Sarah watched her father leave the dining-room door open behind him, expecting her to be following him at any moment. A man of few words on the telephone himself, he disapproved of prolonged conversations even when

someone else was paying for them. She knew he
would have made a note of the time this call started,
especially as he knew it was long-distance.

'Nevertheless I'd much rather be having an early
night with you,' Carlos murmured in her ear. 'Tell
me what time you're planning to go to bed. If I can,
I'll call you again to say goodnight.'

She explained that her room had no telephone.

'I see. Are your family listening in now?' he asked.

'I don't think so, but they are within earshot and
I'll have to explain who's making this long expensive
call from New York.'

'You haven't mentioned me yet?' He sounded
surprised.

'Not yet. Look, I'd better go. There's a guest for
dinner tonight and I think they're waiting to start
eating.'

'Off you go, then. I'll try to call you some time
tomorrow, although the time difference is a compli-
cation. Before noon, your time, I'll be in bed. After
six p.m., New York time, I might be disturbing your
father. If you don't hear from me tomorrow, it's
because I haven't been able to get to a telephone at
a suitable time. Sleep well, sweet Sarah. I'll be
thinking of you. *Adiós*.'

'*Adiós*.'

Disappointed that he hadn't said 'I love you', she
replaced the receiver on its rest and moved with
reluctant steps to join the others.

They had not yet begun to eat.

'Do you realise that telephone call lasted six and
a half minutes?' her father informed her disapprovingly. 'I can't imagine what could be so important
that it couldn't be conveyed by letter at a fraction
of the cost.'

Sarah took her place opposite Jamie. Carlos would

have risen when she entered and drawn out her chair for her, she thought.

'I didn't know you knew anyone in New York,' said Jamie.

'I don't. That was someone I met in Spain who was also on the train from Algeciras. When we reached Paris, he had to rush to catch the Concorde because a relation was critically ill in New York. He rang up to tell me he got there in time.'

'Must have pots of money if he can afford to fly on Concorde,' said Jamie. 'I suppose all the old people down there where your grandmother's living are pretty well-heeled?'

Sarah didn't disabuse him of the idea that she had been speaking of someone elderly. Throughout the meal—a rather dry shepherd's pie with home-grown but overcooked vegetables was followed by stewed apples and custard—she was conscious of missing Carlos and dreading the showdown with Jamie.

The following morning, knowing there was little likelihood of Carlos telephoning before lunch, Sarah drove to the nearest market town to do some errands for Harriet and to buy the current issue of *The Lady* in order to start serious job-hunting.

She had gone to bed upset and exhausted by a painful scene with Jamie, who had reacted to her explanation of her change of heart at first with disbelief and then with anger. Some of the things he had said in the heat of the moment had confirmed what she had long suspected, that deep down he didn't believe in the equality of the sexes and that he had a streak of the bully in him.

It had been a miserable ending to their relationship, but today she felt better for having got the worst part over, even though she knew she hadn't heard the end of it yet. Both sets of parents were going to have plenty to say before the dust finally settled, she felt sure of that.

Looking through the *Wanted* ads while she had a cup of coffee in town, she saw three posts which sounded as if they might suit her. The one she liked best was a job in London, looking after the one-year-old son of a professional couple living in the West End.

She drove home mentally composing her letters of application. As she entered the house by the back door, laden with shopping from the supermarket, Harriet swept into the kitchen.

'Sarah, what is this nonsense about your breaking it off with Jamie? Celia rang up soon after you left. She thinks you must have taken leave of your senses—and so do I!'

Sarah heaved the shopping onto the kitchen table. 'I haven't, Harriet.' she answered quietly. 'In fact I've come to my senses and realised being Jamie's wife wouldn't suit me at all. Please don't try and persuade me to change my mind. I've thought it out very carefully. Nothing you or Mrs Drayton can say will alter my decision. Jamie himself has accepted it. We discussed it for almost two hours after you and Father had gone to play bridge with the Bungays.'

'I wondered why he wasn't here when we got back. I thought it strange . . . until Celia telephoned. She knew something was wrong when he came down to breakfast, looking as if he hadn't slept a wink, she said. It's too bad of you, Sarah. Everyone was expecting the wedding to be announced soon.'

'We weren't even engaged. I can't get married to someone simply because it's expected of me. I'm just not in love with him any more . . . and haven't been for some time.'

'Being in love is much less important than being suited,' snapped Harriet. 'You and Jamie are ideally suited in every way. I can't think what's got into you!'

Her remonstrances, backed by her husband, spoiled Sarah's lunch. They both thought she was out of her mind and would live to regret this apparently sudden volte-face. Nothing she said would convince them the decision wasn't a wilful impulse.

After lunch she escaped to her room to write her letters. The advertisement she preferred asked applicants to write to P Ardsley at a business address in the City. At one time that would have indicated that the child's father was handling the applications, but not any more. Women as well as men worked in the City these days. Sarah began her letter, *Dear Mrs Ardsley* . . . With the two others, and a thank-you letter to her grandmother, it caught the afternoon post.

Carlos telephoned somewhat earlier than he had the previous evening and this time she answered the telephone. He told her his uncle's condition was unchanged and, now that his aunt had the rest of her family with her, Carlos was taking over the handling of the important meetings which had been the reason for the older man's presence in New York.

He sounded preoccupied and said he could spare only a few minutes and might not be able to call her the following day. But the fact that he had made time to call her today, and the sound of his voice, lifted her spirits and fortified her for another of Harriet's homilies at dinner.

The following afternoon, while she was alone in

the house,the telephone rang and she hurried to answer it, hoping it might be Carlos.

A crisp female voice said. 'This is Paula Ardsley. May I speak to Sarah Lancaster, please?'

'Speaking.'

'I have your letter in front of me, Miss Lancaster. Its one of half a dozen replies to our advertisement for a nanny for Alexander, but the only one addressed to me rather than to my husband. For a reason I'll explain when we meet, that's a point in your favour. Can you come to see us on Saturday morning at eleven-thirty?'

'Certainly, Mrs Ardsley.'

'Good. I'll give you our address.'

There had been no further word from Carlos when Sarah set out for London at the weekend. On Paula Ardsley's instructions, she put the car in an underground parking place and walked the short distance to her prospective employers' address.

The door of the tall early nineteenth-century house was opened by a woman in her early thirties wearing a sapphire velour track suit which accentuated the brilliance of her blue eyes. She had auburn hair and some freckles on an ivory skin.

She gripped Sarah's hand. 'I'm Paula Ardsley. Come in. My husband is upstairs in the nursery with Alexander.' Her blue and silver trainers went up the narrows stairs two at a time. She exuded vitality and energy.

Her husband was a quieter, less positive personality. In the hour she spent with them, Sarah learned that he was a partner in an art gallery and Paula was 'something in the City'. They were into role-reversal or perhaps merely role-sharing in other ways, Sarah noticed. It was Tim who made coffee in the well-equipped kitchenette on the nursery floor. The child's bedroom was equipped with a listening device connected to the nanny's bedsitter on the floor above and also to downstairs rooms for when the nanny was off duty. A nice bathroom of her own, a large colour television, an independent telephone . . . the post offered everything a nanny could wish for.

'The snags are the stairs . . . and me,' Paula Ardsley said, with a grin. 'Nanny Castleton, who has just left us by mutual agreement, was Norland-trained and getting on in years. She couldn't take three flights of stairs—four if you count the basement—and she didn't approve of career-mummies, as she called us. It upset her routine. Let me make myself absolutely clear: I'm fighting to get to the top in a man's world and I mean to make it. That involves days when I barely have time to say hello to Alexander. There are other days, like today, when I want to spend a lot of time with him. His nanny has to be flexible, not set in her ways or old-fashioned in her outlook. The fact that you didn't assume P Ardsley at that address *must* be a man suggests that you may be the kind of person I'm looking for.'

By the end of the interview, they had both formed favourable impressions, and Sarah was very taken with the happy-seeming little boy, who took after his father in looks, having brown hair and hazel eyes.

'Right: on Monday I'll check out your references and as soon as that's done I'll get back to you,' said Paula, when they had discussed every aspect of the job. 'You can start right away, I take it?'

Sarah agreed that she could.

Leaving her car where it was, she walked the short distance to the big West End stores where she did some shopping, including buying a dress to wear when next she saw Carlos. It left her funds at a low ebb, so the sooner she started work the better. She knew her references would be satisfactory. The only possible impediment to her going to work for the Ardsleys was if, when she told Carlos, he said, 'Don't commit yourself yet . . . not until I've talked to you.'

Which would mean he wanted to marry her.

There was no call from America that weekend. Nor on Monday or Tuesday. On Wednesday, Colonel Lancaster's *Times* reported the death, the day before, of Lord Hastings, chairman of Hastings Bank, following a second major heart attack while in a New York clinic after a previous coronary. Almost the whole of the newspaper's obituary column was devoted to his life and achievements. The notice concluded with a reference to his widow and two sons.

Later that day Paula Ardsley rang up and arranged for Sarah to arrive at Albion Street on Sunday, to have time to settle in before taking full charge of Alexander on Monday morning, when Paula would be leaving the house at seven o'clock to be at her desk by seven-thirty a.m.

To Sarah's relief, Harriet had suddenly stopped nagging her about Jamie. The subject was no longer mentioned. Instead her stepmother asked questions about Sarah's new employers, making comments indicating that she shared Nanny Castleton's disapproval of career-mummies.

'There hardly seems any point in having a child if

she leaves the house at seven and is out for twelve
hours or longer. I'm surprised her husband puts up
with it.'

'Perhaps he knows that she needs the challenge
and stimulus of a demanding job,' Sarah suggested.

By Friday, not hearing from Carlos had begun to
worry her.

'You will give my London number to anyone who
rings up, won't you?' she said, before leaving home.

'Naturally,' said Harriet.

By early evening, Sarah's cases were unpacked and
put away in the cupboards above the fitted wardrobes
in her pretty peach-and-white room at the top of the
Ardsleys' house.

They had suggested she should call them by their
first names. With Sarah looking on, Paula gave her
son his bath that night, explaining as she did so that
she was a foreign exchange dealer working for the
London office of one of America's largest banks.

'That's why I have to be at work so early . . .
to catch up with overnight currency movements,'
she explained.

From her description of her job, it sounded to
Sarah as if the rewards were high but the pressures
fierce.

With Alexander tucked up and drowsy, they went
down to the comfortable room known as the study
for a drink before dinner. Tim was reclining in an
armchair, his feet on the edge of a low table, reading
one of the Sunday papers.

'I've just been reading this financial columnist's
views on the power struggle in the Hastings board-
room,' he said to his wife. 'Do you agree with his
forecast?'

'Very much so. I think there's no question but that Carlos Hastings will claim the crown . . . and deserves to.' Paula flopped on to one end of the sofa and gestured for Sarah to share it with her. 'I'd like a brandy and Coke, Tim. What about you, Sarah? G and T? Wine? A soft drink?'

'Er . . . wine, please.' Although he had been in her thoughts for much of the day, Sarah had been startled by the reference to Carlos.

'It probably hasn't impinged on you, but one of Britain's top bankers, Lord Hastings, died during the week,' Paula told her. 'Tim has been reading speculations about his successor. He has two sons, one of whom will inherit the title originally given to Maximilian Hastings, the founder of the bank, and also a half-Spanish nephew, all of whom are in line for the chairmanship. The sons are men in their forties. The nephew, Carlos Hastings, is younger . . . mid to late thirties. He used to have the reputation of being a playboy, but recently people have been saying that he's the one who's inherited Maximilian's flair.'

Tim brought his wife her drink, and asked, 'Which colour wine for you, Sarah?'

'White, please.'

'Right: coming up.' Following on Paula's remarks, he continued, 'The nephew is certainly the only one who takes after Maximilian as a connoisseur of art. Every time we put on a new exhibition, I send him a card and a catalogue but we've never managed to lure him into the gallery. He spends a lot of money with our competitors. I wish he'd patronise us.'

'Find something superb and he will,' said Paula. 'That kind of man is only interested in the best, whether it's a car, a horse, a painting . . . or a woman.'

Sarah's first week in her new job would have been happy but for the realisation that it would soon be a fortnight since she had heard from Carlos.

The two other members of Paula's back-up team, as she called them, were Elsie Woody, born and bred near the Edgware Road, who came in to clean on Mondays, Wednesdays and Fridays; and Julia Fleetwood, the widow of an orchestral violinist, who came on Tuesdays and Thursdays to cook for the freezer and refrigerator, and also to do the flowers and any special shopping which was necessary. If, on Saturdays, Paula was giving a dinner party, the planning and most of the preparations were done by Mrs Fleetwood, who would also come in to help on the night.

By Friday, Sarah was beginning to feel anxious and worried. However busy he was in the aftermath of his uncle's death, surely Carlos must have had time to ring her by now? She had read in the paper that Lord Hastings' body had been flown back to England for a private family funeral to be followed at a later date by a public memorial service. It was possible Carlos had remained in America on business, but it seemed unlikely.

She knew he had a flat in London, but he hadn't said where and his telephone number was ex-directory. As she couldn't contact him at home, she decided to go to the head office of the bank, making the return of the hamper the pretext for her visit.

Not that a pretext should be necessary, considering the terms on which they had parted, she thought.

Probably Mrs Woody would have kept an eye on Alexander for an hour but, being so new to her post, Sarah thought it better not to ask her. She took the little boy with her, wheeling him down to Bayswater Road in his push-chair, there to wait for a taxi to take them to the City.

Built in Victorian times, the headquarters of the bank was an impressive edifice inspired by a Greek temple outside and an Italian *palazzo* inside. A man in morning dress with a red carnation in his button-hole was on duty at a desk just inside the main banking hall with its marble columns rising to the gilded balustrades of an upper floor, the whole lit by a glass dome.

'Yes, madam?' he said courteously, as she approached him.

'I've come to return this hamper to Mr Hastings . . . Mr Carlos Hastings. Is he here today?'

'I'll find out for you, madam. Your name is . . . ?'

'Sarah Lancaster.'

After a brief conversation on an internal telephone, he rose and asked her to follow him to a part of the building where the floor was carpeted and heavy mahogany doors hinted at the dignified offices of senior members of the staff.

In a waiting area of considerable grandeur, he said, 'If you would wait here, someone will come to attend to you.'

Sarah didn't sit down. She was too keyed up. Would it be Carlos who came? Possibly displeased by her intrusion into this world of high finance which seemed such an unlikely setting for the Carlos she knew, the horseman, the polo-player, knowledgeable companion of that day in Madrid, the ardent lover who had murmured 'Must you go?' that night on the train to Paris.

Sitting placidly in his push-chair, her charge looked up and burbled an unintelligible comment on the strangeness of his surroundings.

Her troubled expression lightened. She smiled and nodded. 'I agree, Alexander.'

A woman appeared; middle-aged, pleasant-faced, dressed with unobtrusive elegance.

'Mrs Lancaster? I'm Elizabeth Kelling, Mr Hastings' secretary. You have something for him, I believe?'

'Yes . . . but I'm not Mrs Lancaster,' Sarah corrected her. 'I'm Alexander's nanny, not his mother.'

'Oh, I see. I beg your pardon.'

'Is Mr Hastings busy?'

'I'm afraid he is at the moment. He's in a meeting and doesn't want to be disturbed unless it's a matter of great urgency.'

'I see. In that case I'll leave this hamper with you. It belongs to Mr Hastings. I—I expect he'll ring up when he isn't so busy. I'm not at the number he rang before from New York—I'm working in London now. Shall I give you my new number?'

Mrs Kelling had a notebook and pencil in her hand. She wrote it down and, with it, Sarah's address.

'Thank you for returning the hamper, Miss Lancaster. I'll show you out. The corridors can be rather confusing. What a dear little boy. How old is he?'

Making polite small-talk, she escorted Sarah back to the main hall.

Returning to Albion Street in another taxi, the child cuddled on her lap, Sarah felt close to tears. To have been in the same building as Carlos and not to have seen him was desperately disappointing and frustrating. As soon as his meeting was over, would his secretary tell him about her visit and would he immediately ring up, demanding to know where she was and when he could see her? Or, agonising thought, had the meeting been a fabrication, a standard excuse given to people he didn't wish to see or speak to?

All afternoon, while Alexander napped, she waited on tenterhooks, for her telephone to ring. And all evening. And all the next day, Saturday, and Sunday.

By first post on Monday morning came a letter in a thick cream envelope addressed in black ink in an unfamiliar hand. Inside was a single sheet of paper, a continuation sheet with no address on it.

Dear Sarah, she read,

Thank you for returning the hamper.

My uncle's death has left me with many additional responsibilities and less time for personal involvements. I think it best if we don't meet again.

It was initialled *C H.*

She couldn't believe it. For days, she couldn't believe anyone could be so cruel, so heartless.

What had happened? What had changed him from the man who had been gentle, tender, *loving* to the man who had written that brutal note of dismissal?

She remembered his parting kiss at the Gare d'Austerlitz. His first call from New York. *I'd much rather be having an early night with you . . . there are things I want to say to you, but not on the telephone.* Then the second call, brief and preoccupied. Had he already begun to lose interest in her? Had he met someone else? It didn't seem likely when his time must have been spent either at his uncle's bedside, in attendance on his aunt, or taking Lord Hastings' place at meetings with American financiers.

Nobody knew, nobody even suspected the anguish

she went through in the weeks that followed being
'dropped like a hot potato'. She didn't cry, not even
in bed at night. It wasn't the kind of pain which
could be relieved by outbursts of tears. She would
like awake, dry-eyed and desolate, trying to understand how the man she had loved, *still* loved, would
always love, could have banished her from his life
with a curt note.

As the summer passed, it was like the time after
her mother died. She remembered it well; waking up
every morning to the almost instantaneous
knowledge that something terrible had happened,
something which could never be put right.

The heartbreaks of childhood, even the loss of a
parent, did get better in time. Would this? Sarah
didn't think so. As the weeks drew out into months
and summer became an Indian summer and then a
bright autumn, her heart still felt like a lump of lead
in her chest.

Every time Paula mentioned Carlos—and she
mentioned him often, with admiration for the
audacious deals he was pulling off under the noses
of more orthodox merchant bankers—Sarah's pain
was as sharp as before.

'Jacob Rothschild and Carlos Hastings are the
two most interesting, dynamic men in the City . . .
Titans compared with the rest,' said Paula, when
some audacious coup by the Hastings Bank, too
complex for either her husband or nanny to grasp,
had made headlines in the FT, as she called the
Financial Times.

Living in, as she did, Sarah was privy to aspects
of the Ardsleys' marriage not known to outsiders.
Sometimes, usually late at night, they had blazing
rows or, to be more precise, Paula blazed, and next
morning when Tim came up to the nursery to cuddle

his son before going to the gallery, he looked tired and harassed.

They appeared to be an ideal couple, melding two disparate working lives into an enviable domestic lifestyle. Much of the time they were happy. But there were strains under the surface. The gallery's profits were variable. It was Paula's salary, and the huge bonuses she earned from successful deals, which paid for the weekend cottage in the country, the smoked salmon and champagne, the designer clothes. Sarah didn't think Tim minded his wife's income outstripping his, but she sensed he was constantly worried that Paula might not be able to stand the long hours and taxing pace indefinitely and would be dissatisfied with a less lavish standard of living.

One day, not long before Christmas, pushing a well-muffled Alexander along Connaught Street, Sarah paused to look in the window of the antiquarian bookshop which also sold prints. The first thing to catch her eye was a print, originally perhaps an illustration from a Victorian book, of five men playing polo. Four were Indians in turbans and the fifth was a British Army officer wearing a solar topee and sporting a curly moustache. Even if he hadn't looked a bit like Carlos, the print would have reminded her of him.

There were so many reminders. The clip-clop of a police horse's hooves . . . the sleek shape of a Porsche . . . the voice of a Spanish tourist in the Marble Arch Marks & Spencer . . . black hair . . . the taste of olives . . . passing the Ritz Hotel . . . carnations in a florist's window . . . her Spanish sandals, now at the back of the wardrobe behind her winter shoes.

The Ardsleys were spending Christmas at a villa in the south of France with two other couples, one of whom had an older nanny who didn't mind being on duty over the holiday. Sarah and the other young nanny were given a four-day break. On Christmas Eve, with her father and Harriet, she attended a party given by Dr and Mrs Drayton to celebrate Jamie's engagement to a young woman doctor he had met in September.

During the evening, his mother found an opportunity to say to Sarah, 'As you know, I was upset when you and Jamie split up, but it's all worked out for the best. Margaret is a charming girl and of course they have everything in common.'

While appearing to be affable, she managed to convey that Jamie had had a lucky escape. As perhaps he had, thought Sarah, her confidence at a low ebb.

Her married brother was spending Christmas with his in-laws and her other brother was doing voluntary service overseas. She missed them. As her father and Harriet were not people who made much of Christmas, and would have been content on their own, she would have been happier spending a few days with her grandmother. She hadn't suggested it for fear Carlos might also have decided to spend Christmas in the sun. She wasn't ready, and didn't think she ever would be, to risk an accidental encounter with him.

One night in February, in her room, she was flipping through one of Paula's glossy magazines while half-watching a not very riveting programme on television, when a photograph of him made her give a gasp of shock.

He was the tallest of four men all dressed in white riding-breeches with leather pads strapped to their knees. Instead of wearing the usual short-sleeved polo shirts, their sleeves were long and *Cartier* was

printed across their chests. In the background was
an alpine village and pine trees powdered with snow.

Although puzzled by what a polo team was doing
in a setting more appropriate to skiing, Sarah studied
the picture for a long time before turning her attention to the text. One of the men, presumably the
team's captain, was holding a trophy in the form of
a silver model of a horse. He and two others were
smiling. Carlos was looking rather grim.

When she read the extended caption, she learned
that he had been playing in a winter tourament at
St Moritz sponsored by Cartier, the international
jewellers.

Downstairs, on a desk in the study, Tim kept a
powerful magnifying glass for looking at portrait
miniatures and details of larger paintings. The
Ardsleys were out that night and the lower floors
were in darkness when Sarah took the magazine
downstairs to study the photograph more closely.

Enlarged by the strong lens, the tanned raw-boned
face she remembered so well looked older and
somewhat haggard. She thought of the note he had
sent her, which she been unable to bring herself to
destroy. Were his greater responsibilities as the new
chairman of the bank the cause of that drawn look?
Evidently they didn't prevent him from maintaining
his skill at polo. The caption said . . . *the big
scorer in both matches was Carlos Hastings, who was
also in St Moritz to compete for the Brabazon Trophy
on the Cresta Run.*

Sarah wondered if he had won it, and if a beautiful
girl had been there to celebrate with him.

How could she ever have thought she had the
looks, the brains or the charm to hold a man who
excelled at everything he did? A man who, as Paula

had once said, looked for the best whether in horses or women.

Next day, she asked Paula if she could tear a page out of her magazine.

'Go ahead. I've finished with it,' said her employer.

Sarah put the page in the drawer where she kept his note. She was annoyed with herself for wanting to keep the photograph. It was as foolish as a reformed smoker keeping a packet of cigarettes. Sooner or later she would be tempted to look at it again, keeping alive a flame much better extinguished.

At last the long winter merged with a wet spring. But at least the trees were in bud and buckets of massed narcissi and daffodils stood on the pavement outside the Connaught Street flower shop.

Susan, who was Sarah's closest friend among the many other nannies in the area, finally persuaded her out of her self-imposed seclusion. She agreed to join a birthday dinner party consisting of Susan and her current boy-friend Mike, a couple who were engaged, and a friend of Mike's who had recently come to London and didn't know anyone.

'If you don't like him, you don't have to see him again,' Susan had said, coaxing her to join them. 'Do come, Sarah. Whatever happened to turn you off guys—and I'm not trying to pry into something you obviously don't want to take about—it's bad for you *never* to go out except by yourself to the theatre.'

Sarah had bought nothing new since the dress, still unworn, she had bought on the day of her interview. Ever since then she had made do with clothes she already had. Except for essential expenses such as toothpaste and shampoo, and the price of occasional tickets to the theatre or concerts, she had saved nearly all her salary and, advised by Paula, in an account which earned interest.

Having started to make money work for her, she was disinclined to spend much on clothes for a blind date which might not work out. Nor could she bring herself to wear the dress she had bought for Carlos. Nothing else in her wardrobe was suitable for dinner at the 'in' Kensington bistro where the party was being held.

When she consulted Paula about what sort of clothes would look right in that setting, her employer said, 'Separates have more mileage than dresses. Your bottom half won't be noticed. A stunning top is the important thing. As usual at this time of year, the shop will be full of high summer stuff while we're still wearing coats and sweaters. Why not borrow something of mine? We're the same size. Come and look through my things.'

At first Sarah had resisted the suggestion in case she spilt something on an expensive outfit. Paula had her clothes cleaned at Jeeves, the top dry-cleaning firm around the corner, and even that cost an arm and a leg. However, Paula had overruled her objections. One of her cupboards was reserved for clothes waiting to be taken to the dress agency that sold her casts-off at prices which still seemed high to Sarah, who had several times delivered a parcel of them.

So it was a straight black skirt, split at one side, with Yves St Laurent's label inside the waistband, and a creamy silk shirt from the Chanel shop in Bond Street, that hung on the door of Sarah's wardrobe as she made up her face for Susan's birthday dinner.

Her hair, newly washed, had grown out of the deliberate tangle she had worn it in last year and

how was straight and sleek, the ends flipped under
with the electric curling comb Paula had given her
for Christmas. Her own contributions to her 'look'
for tonight were a padded black velvet Alice band
and black lace tights. The total effect, she thought,
when she was ready, was not bad. It was a pity she
couldn't whip up any enthusiasm for meeting Mike's
friend. For Susan's sake she must try to like him,
try to sparkle.

Paula and Tim were not going out that evening.
Alexander was already asleep and Paula was in her
bedroom, doing her nails and waiting for Tim who
had been delayed at the gallery, when Sarah looked
in to say goodbye.

'You look great. Have a good time.' Paula waggled
wet fingertips at her.

Halfway down the stairs to the hall, Sarah heard
Tim unlocking the front door. But it was another
man who enter the house ahead of him. As she
recognised him, she froze. It couldn't be Carlos . . .
but it was. What was he doing here?

Her instinctive reaction was to turn tail and run
up the stairs before he noticed her. But her legs
refused to obey her brain. She stayed rooted to the
spot.

Moments later, it seemed to Sarah, she was in the
back of the taxi which had brought the two men to
the house and it was all over, the mind-numbing,
heart-churning encounter with the man who, this
time last year, had given her a glimpse of heaven
and then plunged her into hell.

Shattered by the unexpected confrontation, Sarah
sank into a corner of the wide leather seat, her
whole body beginning to shake with delayed reaction.

If only she had left the house ten minutes earlier, she wouldn't have met him and wouldn't be in this state. It was only a short drive to her destination. Could she pull herself together in time to present a calm front to Susan and her other guests?

Suddenly, for the first time in the long months of humiliation, pain and despair, she was angry. How dared he not recognise her . . . or pretend not to recognise her? How dared he stay calm and unmoved while she was shaken to the core? How dared he say 'Enjoy yourself' when he—callous, cold-hearted beast—had inflicted a year of year of misery on her?

As the taxi sped westwards through the teeming spring rain, all the passive, negative, *abject* responses she had felt since reading his note were swept aside by an upsurge of fierce indignation.

She was almost impelled to lean forward and ask the driver to take her back to the house, there to storm in and tell Carlos what she thought of him. Then she realised that for Tim he was an important client, one long sought after and badly needed at present when the gallery wasn't doing well. She couldn't upset Tim's applecart for the satisfaction of venting her outrage. Nor could she delay Susan's party.

Sunday was Sarah's day off, but as she was awake at her usual time and heard Alexander making where-is-everybody? noises in his cot in the room below, she went down to keep him amused until one of his parents appeared.

'Oh, I'm sorry . . . I've spoiled your lie-in,' said Paula, coming in, yawning, a few minutes later. 'I heard him shouting on the inter-com, but he woke me out of a deep sleep. It took me five minutes to get myself together. What a rotten mummy you've got yourself, Alexander. I really am sorry, Sarah. How was the party? What time did you get in?'

'Not very late. We went back to Susan's place and then Mike's friend walked me home. About one, I suppose.'

'We must only just have gone to bed. What was Mike's friend like? Nice?'

'Very. I'm going out with him next Saturday.'

'Good . . . I'm glad to hear it.' Like Susan, Paula had never pried into the reasons for Sarah's reclusiveness. 'We had an expected visitor last night—well, you know that. You met him briefly, Tim said.'

'Very briefly,' Sarah agreed, trying to sound as if she hadn't paid much attention to the man Tim had introduced as she was leaving the house.

'What you probably didn't realise was that *that* was the Chairman of Hastings Bank . . . the big fish Tim has been hoping to net for ages,' Paula told her. 'Tim and Tina had almost finished hanging the new show which opens on Monday night when who should turn up but Carlos Hastings, wanting a pre-preview, wily man. Not only has he bought the two most important paintings, but when Tim mentioned the bronzes he's keeping for the next show, Carlos insisted on coming back here to see them and he stayed to have supper with us. As you can imagine, Tim's cock-a-hoop with delight. It's the big boost he needs.'

That's marvellous . . . great,' said Sarah, unable to resist adding, 'What did you think of Mr Hastings?'

'You saw him! Didn't you think he was gorgeous?' Taking Sarah's reply for granted, Paula went on, 'I think he's a walking example of the unfairness of life. Does anyone, born into that family, need those looks and that charm?'

'Looks and charm can be skin-deep. He may be a swine under the glossy surface,' Sarah said lightly.

'I'd be prepared to risk it . . . if I were single. As well as being a godsend to Tim, I think he may be interested in me. Not personally, of course—professionally. He wanted to know about my career to date. I think, unlike most English bankers, he doesn't have a mental block about giving women key jobs. He's spent a lot of time in America where they are more enlightened,' said Paula.

She went on singing his praises until Sarah could stand no more and cut short the eulogy with, 'If you'd like an extra hour in bed, I'll look after Alexander. I've no special plans for today.'

'No, no . . . I've woken up now. I'll get him dressed. I think we should have Buck's Fizz for breakfast this morning; to celebrate Tim's success . . . and also the strong possibility that I may now be in line for a new job at Hastings Bank,' Paula said jubilantly.

The next day Tim's widowed mother came to stay with them and went to the private view which was an outstanding success with several prospective buyers frustrated by Carlos Hastings stealing a march on them.

On Tuesday morning the senior Mrs Ardsley said it would give her great pleasure to take Alexander for his push-chair tour of the park. They had only been gone a short time, and Sarah was in the basement kitchen, chatting to Mrs Fleetwood, when the doorbell rang.

'I'll go.' Sarah ran up the stairs to the hall.

She was wearing jeans and a tee-shirt, her usual rig in the morning. Expecting the man who was coming to service the nursery washing-machine, she was starting to smile when she opened the door.

The friendliness in the grey eyes changed to startled displeasure when she saw who was waiting outside.

'I'm afraid neither Mr nor Mrs Ardsley are at home this morning,' she said coldly.

'I didn't come to see them. It's you I want to talk to,' said Carlos. 'May I come in?'

Although on Saturday night she would have given a great deal for a chance to upbraid him, now she found herself stammering, 'I—we have nothing to say to each other . . . *Mr* Hastings.'

'I think we have.'

When she would have shut the door, he put the flat of his hand on the centre panel, holding it open with the muscular power of the arm accustomed to swinging a polo mallet.

Her temper began to kindle. 'How dare you force your way in here! I'm not alone—Mrs Fleetwood is downstairs.'

'I haven't forced my way in yet. I am merely preventing you from slamming the door in my face; an ungracious act which I'm sure wouldn't have the approval of your employers who made me most welcome,' he answered smoothly.

'They don't know what a rat you are!' she retorted hotly.

'Or what a liar you are!' His face was suddenly taut with angry contempt and he spoke with a snap she had never heard in his voice before.

'I don't know what you mean,' she said, in genuine bewilderment.

'Then I'll tell you, but not here—inside.'

As he made to cross the threshold, instinctively

Sarah shrank back and allowed him to come in. She had seen Carlos Hastings in several moods, all of them fundamentally affable. Now the mask of amused charm was off, revealing the face of a man with a much fiercer temper than hers burning in his dark Spanish eyes, and the wide sensual mouth which had kissed her set in a punitive line.

CHAPTER SIX

'YOU'D better go through to the study . . . the door at the far end,' said Sarah, as Carlos stepped into the hall and waited for her to close the door.

She guessed that the Ardsleys would have entertained him in the drawing-room on Saturday. The drawing-room was Paula's showpiece; two rooms made into one and done out by Colefax & Fowler, a leading and very expensive firm of interior decorators who had made it a perfect setting for Tim's ever-changing collection of paintings, and for impressing the 'top people' she aspired to join.

Carlos strode towards the door she indicated, and it was a measure of the mood he was in that he opened it and walked through rather standing aside for her to precede him.

Sarah followed, torn between fury at his outrageous accusation that she was a liar and fear of what he might do if they had a stand-up fight. Once she had thought she knew him—and had discovered she didn't. Now she was very much aware that he had sides to his nature of which she knew nothing; including his temper.

At least, as she had warned him, she wasn't alone. Julia Fleetwood was downstairs and could be summoned by turning one of the old-fashioned bell levers which were a period feature of the house.

In the study Carlos went straight to the window which overlooked the back garden, a narrow walled space 'landscaped' by a garden designer and serviced twice a month.

His shoulders had never looked broader than they did as he stood with his back to her, his tall frame silhouetted against the light. As soon as he heard the door close, he swung round.

By this time Sarah had decided not to be intimidated. Thrusting her fingers into the pockets of her jeans and lifting her chin, she said coldly, 'Now perhaps you'd explain what you mean by calling me a liar. Considering the absolutely contemptible way you've behaved, I——'

'You lied by default,' he cut in. 'Which is as bad as a direct lie.'

'I still don't know what you're talking about.'

'You let me think you were free when in fact you were engaged.'

'I was never engaged. Where did you get that idea?'

'The day I flew back to England for a few hours and drove down to see you, only to find you were in London for an interview . . . presumably with the Ardsleys. But it wasn't a wasted trip, in fact it was very illuminating. Your stepmother told me what you had omitted to mention; that you were engaged to the son of the local doctor.'

It was not the discovery that Harriet had lied to him which made her look stunned, but that he had been to the house and she had said nothing about it; that while Sarah was beginning to wonder why he hadn't telephoned, he had been there and gone away believing her bound to Jamie.

He must have flown over by Concorde, returning the same day. All that money and all that way just to spend, at the most, an hour with her. There could only be one reason why a man, even a rich man, would rush across the Atlantic, leaving a family crisis, to see a girl. To say things which couldn't be said on the telephone, or not as well. I love you. Will you marry me?

The certainty that he had meant to propose to her, and the memory of all she had suffered in consequence of not being at home that day, brought Sarah's hands out of her pockets and up to her mouth. A small groan of anguish escaped her. Oh, Harriet . . . how could you . . . how could you? was the thought in her mind.

Carlos seemed to take her reaction as an admission of guilt.

'I gather she didn't tell you about our conversation,' he said curtly. 'Well, now you know why I came to my senses about you. God knows I should have been wise to the stratagems of gold-digging females, but you had me fooled for a while. I took you for a nice girl who wouldn't deceive a fly. But you took damn good care not to let on there was someone in England who thought you belonged to him, didn't you?'

'I didn't belong to Jamie,' she protested. 'I had been in love with him once—yes. But it was over by the time I met you.'

'Not according to Mrs Lancaster. She didn't strike me as a woman given to exaggeration. According to her, before your visit to Spain, you and Drayton were planning to marry. Are you suggesting she lied to me?'

Sarah's first feeling that all this was Harriet's fault was beginning to veer to the view that Carlos had judged her, Sarah, on insufficient evidence. If he had had so little faith in her that he hadn't waited to hear her side of the story before writing that cruel 'get lost' note, it didn't say much for the depth or strength of his feelings for her.

'No, I'm not saying she lied . . . merely that whatever she told you was only her view of the matter. I hadn't discussed my feelings with her.'

'So I gathered. You'd led her to believe that my calls from New York were from an elderly man, a contemporary and friend of your grandmother. Obviously you needed time to rid yourself of existing obligations before announcing to your family that you'd found a better fish to fry,' he said caustically.

It was at once close to the truth and very far from it.

'If you're determined to think the worst of me, what can I say?' she asked bitterly. 'Except that I'm sorry for anyone who expects you to trust them. Clearly you don't know the meaning of the word. What's more, I think you're paranoid about women trying to trap you. When I liked you—please note I'm using the past tense—it wasn't because you were rich and important. It was for other reasons . . . although I must admit it's hard to remember what they were,' she added. 'Whatever they were, they were instantly cancelled by that vile note you wrote me. There are girls who, treated like that, would have done something silly like swallowing a bottle of pills. Luckily for you, I'm made of sterner stuff. I just wrote you off as subhuman and was glad I'd found out in time.'

Having said her piece, she found that instead of feeling better she felt as wretched as before, and perilously close to tears.

Carlos was glowering at her. 'You're not wearing a ring.'

'I've told you . . . I was never engaged to Jamie. Next month he's marrying someone else.'

After a pause, he said, 'And you? Is there someone else for you now?'

How can there be? Sarah thought. How can there ever be anyone else for me after our journey together? Are you blind that you can't see I'm still in love with you? And always will be?

Aloud, she said, 'Well, of course. You didn't expect to find me nursing a broken heart, did you? Where did you think I was going on Saturday night? To a hen party?' She shrugged. 'I'm sure there've been plenty more "personal involvements" in your life.'

For a long moment his dark eyes bored into hers. Then he said harshly, 'You were right. We have nothing to say to each other. I don't know why I thought we had. I'll see myself out.'

Later that day, Sarah telephoned Mike's friend Stephen, to say she was sorry but something had come up and she would have to cancel their date for next Saturday night because she needed to go home for the weekend.

She couldn't detect any serious disappointment in his voice. As soon as they met she had seen that he wasn't the type to be lonely in London for long. She suspected that Susan and Mike had pressed him to ask her out and he, being an obliging young man and finding her not unattractive, had not been averse.

'Some other weekend maybe? I'll give you a buzz,' was his cheerful parting remark.

As she couldn't keep the Lancia in London, she went home by coach from Victoria and was met at the other end by her father. She had left London early and was home in time for lunch.

Afterwards all three of them spent the afternoon

gardening. It wasn't until later, while helping with
the supper preparations in which her father took no
part, that Sarah said, 'Why didn't you tell me Carlos
Hastings came here the day I went to London,
Harriet?'

A bright flush of discomfiture suffused her
stepmother's face. 'I—I saw nothing to be gained by
it,' she answered. 'It seemed to me he had already
caused you to behave very foolishly. It was obvious
that he was behind your changed attitude to Jamie.
How did you find out he came here?'

'He told me. Last weekend he bought some paintings from Tim's new exhibition. Tim brought him
home. Didn't it cross your mind that you had no
right to interfere in my life? Have you any idea of
the unhappiness you've caused me?'

Harriet avoided her eyes. 'I did what I thought
was best. If you hadn't lost your head over him, you
might be married to Jamie . . . comfortably
settled . . . secure.'

'If you hadn't told Carlos a lie I might now be
married to him and blissfully happy,' said Sarah,
her heart wrenched by the thought of what now
could never be.

'He wouldn't have married you,' said Harriet. 'He
would have persuaded you to have an affair with
him. I've seen it happen before. Good-looking older
men . . . silly infatuated girls. You say I caused
you unhappiness. If you did but know it, I may have
spared you much greater misery. He would have
kept you on a string for as long as it suited him and
then you would have found yourself discarded. It's
what invariably happens with men of that sort.'

'How can you say that? You don't know anything
about him.'

'I saw his car. I saw him . . . and the flowers he

brought you . . . the presents from New York. That's the way they always go about things . . . sweeping girls off their feet with extravagant gifts. It's a different story when they begin to lose interest.'

Suddenly, to Sarah's astonished dismay, Harriet's mouth puckered and her eyes brimmed with tears. She fumbled in the pocket of her apron for a handkerchief. 'I—I wanted to save you from going through what happened to me,' she said, in an unsteady voice. She pressed the handkerchief to her lips and closed her eyes. But the tears squeezed between her lids and trailed down her cheeks.

'Harriet!' Sarah hurried round the table, pulled out a chair and steered her stepmother into it.

She had never been fond of her and, since Carlos's revelation, had felt considerable hostility towards her. But her nature was too warm-hearted for her to maintain that attitude in the face of this sudden breakdown.

'What happened to you?' she asked, with an arm round her shoulders.

So then, between sniffs and sobs, it all came out: Harriet's unsuspected past. The quiet, conscientious, rather prim girl working her way up from the typing-pool to become the boss's secretary, at the same age Sarah was now, and then attracting the attention of the boss's nephew who, having nothing better to do at the time, had seen her primness as a challenge.

'Poor you . . . I had no idea,' said Sarah, still faintly incredulous when the sad little saga of infatuation, seduction and finally rejection had been recounted and Harriet was beginning to regain control of herself.

'I—I wouldn't have told you except to prove that I *know* what it's like to have one's head turned by flattery and extravagant attentions,' the older woman said, with a shaky sigh.

'I'll make you a cup of tea.' Sarah went to fill the kettle.

She couldn't say to her stepmother: But all that was twenty-five years ago, when the world was a different place and you, by your own admission, were exceptionally clueless about men.

By the time they sat down for their evening meal, Harriet had bathed her eyes with cold water and showed little trace of her emotional outburst. Sarah had a feeling the subject would never be referred to again and Harriet would always believe her lie to Carlos had been justified.

However, later that night her stepmother knocked on her door shortly after Sarah had climbed into bed and started reading. She knew it was Harriet by the diffident tap-tap instead of her father's firm rap on the rare occasions when he had come to her room.

'Come in.'

Harriet entered, looking uncertain of her welcome. 'Am I disturbing you?'

The straight answer was Yes, but Sarah forbore to make it and said politely, 'Not at all. That's a new dressing-gown, isn't it?'

'It was a birthday present from your father.' Harriet perched on the foot of the divan. 'Are you still unhappy over that man . . . Charles Hastings?'

Sarah didn't correct her. 'I'm getting over it.' She didn't want a heart-to-heart.

'It's a pity you've met him again. It's easier to forget people when you don't see them. You'll meet someone else one day, Sarah . . . someone kind and good and reliable like your father. Those are the qualities to look for in a husband, not looks and charm and money.'

Sarah considered various answers. Do you think it's impossible for a man to be charming *and* good? It depends what you want out of life; I don't want my marriage to be primarily a refuge, with no excitement or passion in it.

After a pause, she said, 'Yes, I know that. Don't worry about me, Harriet. I'm in no hurry to settle down. I have a good job and there are plenty more waiting when my time with Alexander runs out. I may not get married for years yet.'

'You don't want to leave it too late if you're going to have babies of your own.'

Sarah didn't show what she was thinking: Do go away or I'll start to get angry again. She simulated a yawn.

Mercifully Harriet took the hint. 'You're tired and Philip will be wondering where I am. Goodnight, my dear.'

'Goodnight.'

When the door had closed, Sarah didn't immediately resume reading. She lay thinking about her future, knowing that if she didn't see Carlos for ten years she would never be able to forget him.

She returned to London to find Paula in great excitement over an invitation to a party Carlos was giving at his flat in a few days' time.

'Where is his flat?' asked Sarah, unable to repress her curiosity.

'It's the top floor of one of the converted warehouses on this side of the Thames upstream from Tower Bridge. I bet it's fabulous,' said Paula. 'What d'you think I should wear? My new Krizia outfit with the sparkly bustier, or the silk print from Feathers?'

On the night she decided on the white crêpe Krizia three-piece. It was a black-tie party. Seeing Tim in his dinner jacket reminded Sarah of the time Carlos had called at Molly Grantham's flat on his way to a party at Marbella. Would it have been better for her if she had never seen him again?

She knew it was foolish but, after the Ardsleys had left the house, she felt like Cinderella, left alone by the kitchen hearth, after everyone else had gone to Prince Charming's ball. As they always did when they went out, they had given her the number where they could be located in an emergency. Tim had also written down the East End address, once a dockside area of London where only the poor lived but now a fashionable neighbourhood with property values rocketing.

If she had known his address and had gone to see Carlos at home, instead of calling at the bank, would it have made any difference? she wondered. Might he have listened to her explanation of the truth about her relationship with Jamie? His belief that she had deliberately misled him must still rankle or why had he come to see her, to accuse her to her face of lying to him?

The irony of it was that now she *had* told him a lie by claiming to have someone else in her life. She wished she hadn't said that. Not that it made any difference. She wouldn't be seeing him again. If Paula invited him to her next dinner party, as undoubtedly she would, Sarah would have no occasion to go downstairs while he was in the house.

It being a weekday, Paula left the house at her usual

time the next morning. The first report of the party
came from Tim, who came up to the nursery
complaining of a headache.

'Was it a good party?' asked Sarah.

'Yes, I can't blame our host for my hangover. The
food was excellent, the wines even better, and there
was a very interesting mix of people. As for the flat
and the things in it—fantastic!' he told her.

Without being asked, Paula filled in the details
when she came home that evening.

'It was the most sumptuous buffet I've ever seen.
My God, that man knows how to live! Everything
in the place was a collector's piece, but the effect
wasn't museumy like the homes of some of Tim's
customers. It was very relaxed and comfortable, and
the views up and down the river at night are
beautiful . . . as they must be by day. I don't
know why we never thought of looking for a place
in that area. It would be much more convenient for
me, if not for Tim.'

'Does Mr Hastings have a girl-friend?' Sarah
asked.

'If he does, she wasn't there last night. All the
women had husbands and I didn't pick up any signs
that one of them might be Carlos's current mistress.
It wasn't a very large party. I counted eleven couples,
including ourselves, and Tim and I were the
youngest . . . and the least distinguished,' Paula
added. 'To be honest, we didn't fit in. Everyone was
charming to us and we both felt at ease, but I had
the feeling we'd replaced a couple who'd dropped
out, or that he'd included us as an afterthought. He
did say, when he rang me up, that it was very short
notice. Anyway, it's put Tim on the map with some
important people, and it means I can give a dinner
party for Carlos and put him on my right where I

can talk to him for longer and impress him with my potential.'

The following week, Mrs Fleetwood said to Sarah, 'This dinner party Mrs Ardsley is giving on the twentieth is something special, I gather? I've had instructions to buy the best caviar which, for ten people, is going to cost more than the rest of the meal including the wine. I don't think it's worth it myself.'

'I've never tried it,' said Sarah.

'It's nice, but I wouldn't pay the king's ransom it costs nowadays. Who's coming that night? Do you know?'

'A banking VIP, I believe.'

'Ah, I see. It's not just a social occasion but perhaps a step up the ladder. She's having the flowers done professionally but leaving the meal to me,' said Mrs Fleetwood.

Sarah sensed she was hurt that Paula did not consider her flower arrangements good enough for the occasion.

The wine for the dinner party was the subject of one of the rows which blew up from time to time. Sarah heard Paula storming at Tim in their bedroom and, next day, was told the reason. Paula wanted to serve vintage champagne at the dinner party, but Tim thought it an unnecessary expense.

So did Sarah, but she didn't say so. Going round the booths at the *feria,* Carlos hadn't cavilled at drinking *vino de pasto,* ordinary wine. She thought him the last man to be impressed by conspicuous extravagance. Nor did she wish to take sides in a domestic tiff. She avoided giving her opinion by asking if Paula had decided what to wear.

The day before the dinner party, Mrs Fleetwood rang up to say her son-in-law was in hospital following a serious road accident. She was sorry to let Mrs Ardsley down, but her daughter needed her in Leeds.

Sarah saw nothing to be gained by ringing Paula at work. When Tim came home, she told him what had happened.

'If Paula can't get anyone else to take over, I think I could cope, at a pinch,' she offered.

'Could you? That would be super. Paula will go berserk if anything goes wrong with this dinner party. It's very important to her.'

When his wife came home later, she was annoyed that Sarah hadn't rung her immediately, giving her more time to contact professional caterers.

'Why not let Sarah take over?' said Tim. 'Mrs Fleetwood has organised everything. It's largely a matter of heating things up and serving them.'

In the event, Paula had no option but to rely on Sarah because she couldn't find anyone else to step into the breach at such short notice.

If the guests had all been unknown to her, Sarah would have enjoyed her unaccustomed role as cook-cum-parlourmaid. She did not have to worry about replenishing the wine glasses. Tim who, rather unexpectedly, had put his foot down on the matter of the vintage champagne, saw that everyone was well supplied with the white and red wines he had chosen. He also helped Sarah to remove the plates at the end of each course, an assistance which might not meet with Paula's approval but for which Sarah was grateful.

'Well done: you're a brick,' he said, coming into the kitchen when the main course was over and everything, so far, had gone smoothly.

'Thanks for your help. I can manage single-handed

from now on. You stick to your duties as host,' she told him, smiling.

Paula had decided it would be a sophisticated touch to copy the French and serve the cheese before the pudding. She herself was eating very little, concentrating her attention on the two men on either side of her, particularly Carlos.

From the snatches of conversation she overheard each time she circled the table, it seemed to Sarah that he wasn't taking as active a part in the conversation as he had when dining at the Cortijo Los Canos. Each time she offered him something, she kept her eyes on the serving dish but was intensely conscious of his nearness and of his quiet 'Thank you', a courtesy neglected by some of the other guests who behaved as if a robot were serving them. Sarah never looked directly at him and told herself she was imagining that she felt him looking at her. Why should he?

By the time she had brought in the pudding and subsequently cleared the table for coffee, which Paula wanted served in the dining-room, she was beginning to feel tired.

After dashing upstairs to check that Alexander was still sleeping peacefully—the listening device didn't extend to the kitchen—Sarah came down and loaded the pudding plates in the dish-washer.

She was sitting on a stool, eating some left-over chocolate mousse, when, to her confusion, the spring-controlled door swung open and Carlos walked in. As it was too soon for Paula to have led the women up to her bedroom to repair their make-up while the men lingered over port and cigars, he must have made an excuse to leave the dining-room before the female exodus.

Conscious that she was beginning to wilt and,

while upstairs, should have taken a few minutes to touch up her own make-up, Sarah said, 'Am I wanted in the dining-room?' How odd of Paula to send him to fetch her.

Carlos shook his head. 'I noticed you'd burned your wrist. Let me see it.'

'It's nothing . . . a tiny burn. I ran the cold tap on it.'

She extended her wrist to display the small red patch of seared skin, not expecting him to take hold of her hand and elbow while he examined it. His touch had the same effect as it had had in Spain. If anything, it was more disturbing.

He said, 'I thought you were the Ardsleys' nanny, not head cook and bottlewasher as well.'

'I'm not. I'm just helping out in an emergency.'

'To be on your feet all evening as well as all day is too much. You look tired out.' He still held her fingers in his, his other hand cupped under her elbow.

'I'm fine.' Sarah didn't look up at him for fear he would see in her eyes just what his touch did to her.

There were voices in the hall. The women guests were on their way upstairs. Again the kitchen door opened. This time it was Tim who came in.

'Oh . . . ' He looked surprised to see Carlos whom, no doubt, he had assumed to be in the downstairs cloakroom.

'Miss Lancaster has slightly injured herself in the course of producing that excellent meal,' said his tall guest.

'It's nothing,' Sarah repeated. 'A minute burn . . . nothing to fuss about.'

Tim looked at it and agreed with her. 'I came in to thank you for holding the fort for us, Sarah, and to make sure you go off duty now. You've done

more than enough. Leave everything else for Mrs
Woody to clear up in the morning,' he told her.

'All right, I'll do that. Thank you.' She rose from
the stool. For the first time since he had come into
the room she looked up at Carlos. 'Goodnight, Mr
Hastings.'

It was difficult to interpret his expression. That it
was kinder than the basilisk glare she remembered
from their row in the study did not, perhaps, mean
very much. A good meal and plenty of wine mellowed
anyone.

'Goodnight.'

He and Tim left the kitchen where, in spite of
Tim's instructions, she did some more clearing up to
occupy herself until she heard the women coming
downstairs.

When the coast, in this case the hall, was clear,
she took a tray of left-overs and a half-full bottle of
wine up to her room. It would have been nice, she
thought, if before disappearing into the drawing-
room Paula had put her head round the kitchen
door to say a brief word of thanks. On the other
hand, it was natural that she should be preoccupied
with her role as hostess. No doubt she would repair
the omission tomorrow.

It was almost one o'clock when the dinner party
broke up. Sarah was still awake when she heard
people leaving. Indeed, she wasn't yet in bed but
was sitting at the writing-desk section of the counter
which doubled as a dressing-table, having two knee-
holes between three banks of drawers. The metal
waste bin, papered to match the peach walls, was
full almost to the brim with scrunched-up sheets of
paper, but she had finally finished a four-page letter
to Carlos—*so that you will at least know I'm not a
liar and never wilfully deceived you.*

* * *

'A present from Tim and me to show our appreciation for all the hard work you put in on Saturday
night,' said Paula, handing Sarah a large box when
she got home from the bank on Monday evening.
'It's for your summer holiday,' she added, as Sarah
began to open it.

Inside the box she found a lime-green swimsuit,
with a lime and white wraparound beach skirt and
top, and a large matching quilted cotton beach-bag
which unzipped to form a sunbathing mat with a
blow-up pillow at one end.

'I bought the same set for myself, in a different
colour. For once, I took a long lunch break and
went shopping,' said Paula, after Sarah had thanked
her for the expensive gift. 'A fortnight today we'll
be basking in sunny Spain.'

'Spain?' Sarah queried, puzzled.

The Ardsleys had planned a holiday in late
September, renting a villa in Tuscany with the friends
with whom they had shared Christmas but this time
taking Alexander and Sarah along.

'Carlos Hastings has invited us to take a break at
his place on the Costa del Sol and, by the grace of
heaven, I've managed to swing some extra time off.
I should have taken it anyway. I'm sure this isn't
only a social invitation. I think there'll be other
people there and we're all in the running for some
key job in his organisation. It's an American way of
doing things. Get all the candidates together, get
them relaxed and off guard, and see how they
compare.'

'Rather a nerve-racking "holiday",' said Sarah.

'Only for those who aren't sure they're up to
handling whatever the plum job is. I know I can

handle anything he offers me,' said Paula confi-
dently.

Sarah had thought that by 'we' Paula had meant
herself and Tim. Like him, she didn't realise she was
included in the invitation until he suggested they
ought to get Mrs Woody to sleep in the house during
their absence.

'A week here all on her own with Alexander will
be rather lonely for Sarah,' he pointed out.

'They're both coming with us,' Paula told him.
'Carlos's house won't be a crummy little villa with
hardly room to swing a cat. I expect it'll be the
ultimate in luxury. Some of his guests may even
bring maids or valets with them. This is the big
league, Timmy.'

'I suppose so.'

Tim's expression suggested to Sarah that he was
perfectly happy in the league he was in and might
be growing jealous of Carlos and Paula's admiration
for him.

She longed to ask if taking Alexander to Spain
had been Paula's idea or her host's. Presumably the
invitation had been given on Saturday night, though
if that were the case it seemed strange that neither
Paula nor Tim had mentioned it on Sunday. Perhaps
it had been a telephone call from Carlos this morning
which had made Paula rush to the shops at lunch-
time instead of staying at her desk with a sandwich
and a glass of orange juice as she usually did except
when she had a client to take to lunch.

Carlos's post this morning, at his private address,
would have included Sarah's letter to him. But, like
many top businessmen, he might go to his office
early and not see his private mail until he returned
to his flat in the evening.

She wondered if he would respond to the letter in

any way, or if, knowing she was going to be at Sotogrande soon, he would wait until then to say something about it. He might even ignore it. Yet if he still despised her and wanted nothing more to do with her, why had he spotted the burn which no one else had noticed, and why had he come to the kitchen and held her arm with the gentleness of which his strong fingers were capable?

That night she telephoned her grandmother to tell her she was coming to Spain, although she couldn't be sure what time off, if any, she would have.

'But I should be able to get one evening off to spend with you, Granny.'

'I hope so, darling. I should be very disappointed not to see something of you while you're so near. Who would have thought the next time you came down you'd be staying with Carlos Hastings? Have you seen anything of him since you were here? I imagine not or you'd have said so in your letters.'

'I've seen him a couple of times since he became friendly with the Ardsleys.' Sarah had described her journey home last year to Mrs Grantham, but without reference to Carlos.

The frontier between Spain and Gibraltar having at last been re-opened, the Ardsleys flew to the Rock where they were met by Carlos, driving a rented Mercedes this time as he had also flown in a few days before.

Tim sat in the front passenger seat and the two women sat in the back with Alexander on Sarah's lap. They had come by an early flight, refusing the meal on the aeroplane because Carlos had said lunch would be waiting for them.

As the hot sun of July burned down on the already

parched-looking landscape between Gibraltar and
Sotogrande, Sarah's thoughts were of the moonlit
drive back from the *feria* and her accident on the
beach soon after sunrise.

Amparo seemed not to recognise Sarah as the girl
Don Carlos had carried into the house. Or perhaps
she had been instructed not to show that she did.
Her manner was polite but reserved, except with
Alexander, whom she insisted on taking from Sarah,
addressing him in doting Spanish as she bounced
him on her arm and patted his cheek. Sarah expected
him to be alarmed, perhaps to cry, but there seemed
to be something about the housekeeper he liked.

Within half an hour of their arrival they had shed
the clothes appropriate to a cool July morning in
London and were having lunch beside the pool,
shaded by a canopy of fine canes. This reduced the
heat and the glare of the hottest hours of the day to
a pleasantly diffused light and a more comfortable
temperature.

No mention was made of any more guests arriving
and throughout lunch it was Tim's background in
which Carlos seemed most interested. After lunch
Sarah took Alexander off for his nap and stayed in
his room, reading a paperback she had bought at
the airport. She felt she ought to keep out of the
way as much as possible. She wasn't really a guest
here, merely a guest's employee who, as such, should
strive to be neither seen nor heard more than was
essential.

When Alexander woke up she rubbed him all over
with high-protection sun-cream, popped a cotton
hat on his head and, wearing her new green swimsuit,
took him for his first swim.

The garden was deserted, the pool still. The

Ardsleys must be resting and perhaps Carlos was also having a siesta.

Alexander loved bath-time and he liked being in a huge outdoor bath with Sarah even more than their usual water-games. Chortling with delight, he kicked and splashed, making her laugh as she dipped him in and out of the sun-warmed water.

Suddenly there was a whooshing sound and his eyes goggled at the sight of the dolphin fountain playing across the surface of the pool. Holding his wriggling little body, Sarah looked round to see who had switched it on. It was Carlos. Having her back to the pavilion and being intent on the child's antics, she had failed to notice him.

He walked round the edge of the pool to where they were. He was wearing a bathing slip and his body was deeply tanned compared with his visitors' pale skins.

Coming down the steps into the water, he said, 'Let me take him while you have a swim.'

'Thank you . . . if he'll go to you.'

It was impossible to pass the child safely from her grasp to his without their hands touching. Alexander didn't mind who held him as long as it wasn't time to come out.

Sarah swam to the deep end where she hoisted herself on to the deck and used the spring-board to launch herself into the shining depths.

When she surfaced, not far from the others, Carlos said, 'You swim well.'

She smoothed back her streaming fair hair. 'I've always liked the water.'

Swishing the child to and fro, he said, 'I thought you'd like to spend your first evening here with your grandmother. I'll drive you over at seven. Amparo will look after this tadpole. She's very fond of small children.'

'So I gathered. I did tell Paula and Tim my grandmother lived near here, but they don't know that you've met her or that I've been to this house before.'

'So I gathered,' he answered. 'By the way, thank you for writing to me.'

Not knowing what to say, she waited for him to give her a lead, but he didn't. When the pause was becoming awkward, she said, 'I—I think Alexander ought to come out now. He has Tim's hair but Paula's complexion. I must take care not to let him stay in the sun too long.'

'And be careful yourself,' said Carlos. 'You are also very fair.'

For an instant he seemed to be looking at her as he had in the Retiro park. But perhaps she was only imagining the warmth in his eyes. Before she could be sure, Tim appeared with his camera.

'Hold it! I want a snap of the flasher in the hat.'

It was Carlos's groom, José-Maria, who drove Sarah back in the Land Rover after her evening with her grandmother.

Don Carlos had taken his other guests to Marbella for dinner, he explained in heavily accented English. They were not expected to return until long after he and Amparo and the *señorita* were asleep.

Paula would love Marbella and its environs, thought Sarah. Strolling along the glitzy waterfront at Puerto Banús, wearing one of her new resort outfits, flanked by two personable men, one of them 'big league', would be her idea of heaven.

Am I jealous of her? she wondered. Not because

Carlos admires her flair as a foreign-exchange dealer, but because he may also be interested in her as a woman . . . as a wife. The fact that she is married to Tim isn't an insuperable obstacle. Big-league people are always changing partners. Does she really love Tim, or has she fallen out of love with him as I did with Jamie? When they married she was a Stock Exchange secretary. She didn't know then she had it in her to become a successful dealer. If she left him, she wouldn't lose Alexander. Tim loves her too much to deny her her son. But losing her would destroy him.

Strangely, although she believed Paula could be tempted to abandon her marriage for an even more high-powered, moneyed lifestyle than the one she already enjoyed, in her heart of hearts Sarah couldn't believe that Carlos was ruthless enough to filch another man's wife because he found her attractive and admired her success in what for so long had been considered a man's world.

She spent a restless night wondering about his motive for inviting the Ardsleys to stay with him. Probably she slept most of the night, but it seemed to her that for much of it she lay awake, wondering and worrying whether, after this holiday, she would be plunged in despair again.

Towards sunrise she rose from the bed and went to the window to look longingly at the swimming pool, its motionless surface reflecting the rose-tinged, gold-streaked dawn sky. But to swim might disturb the rest of the household, as might taking a shower.

Presently she realised that because of the difference between Spanish and and British time, Alexander would be waking an hour later than usual by the clock. She could walk down to the beach,

have a swim in the sea and be back before he began
to clamour for attention.

She ran most of the way to the beach and saw no
one else about. At first, as she waded in, the sea felt
cold. A few minutes later she was floating on her
back, kicking up spray as happily as Alexander in
the pool yesterday.

She would have stayed in the water longer but for
the need to get back before he woke up and disturbed
his elders who, if they hadn't returned from Marbella
until the small hours, probably wouldn't surface
until mid-morning or later.

She had dried and dressed and was towelling her
hair when she heard the familiar sound of a horse
cantering on soft ground. She looked towards
Gibraltar and saw Carlos riding towards her.

'I didn't expect to see you down here at this hour,'
he said, when he had dismounted a few yards away.

'Nor I you. What time did you get back from the
fleshpots?'

'Two o'clock or thereabouts.' He led his mount,
a beautiful pure-bred Arab, up to her. 'Do you
remember the last time we were here?'

'How could I forget?' Sarah said lightly. 'I still
have the scar on my foot.' She rubbed the Arab
under his chin and then stroked his graceful arched
neck.

Carlos said quietly, 'I have a scar on my heart.'

She looked at him, hardly daring to believe she
had heard him correctly.

He confirmed that she had by going on, 'I fell in
love with you that morning—although I didn't know
it was love until later. I think you loved me . . .
for a time. Is it possible that, in spite of what I did
to you, you still do? Can you forgive me, Sarah?'

The appeal in the dark eyes made her dizzy with

joy. 'I—I think if you truly love someone, you can forgive them anything,' she said, in a husky murmur. 'Even a year of terrible unhappiness without them. Do you mean it, Carlos? Do you really love me?'

He caught her to him, straining her tightly against him.

'Mi vida . . . mi corazón!'

My life . . . my heart. It was in his mother's tongue, his own first language, that he poured out his feelings. Sometimes she didn't understand what he was saying between kisses, but not knowing what all the words meant didn't make the sense any less clear. He loved her. The whole purpose of bringing the Ardsleys to Sotogrande had been to try to rekindle the love he knew now he should never have doubted.

'Why *did* you doubt it? Why did you write that horrible note . . . not giving me a chance to defend myself?' she asked. 'Had it something to do with what you once told me . . . that you were a cynic and had reason to be?'

'Yes, it had,' he agreed. 'When I was in my twenties, I had a disillusioning experience with a girl who appeared to love me but dropped me almost overnight when a better prospect, in the form of an American multi-millionaire's son, came her way. Since then I've tended to distrust all women. Also, I suppose, I didn't trust the rapidity of your effect on me. Love at first sight—or even second sight—has always struck me as a nonsense.'

'Dick Francis knew at a glance that a girl he met at a wedding was going to be his wife,' she told him. 'You couldn't call him an un-sensible man.'

'An eminently sane one, I should think.' Carlos took her face between his palms, his thumbs gently stroking the smoothness of her cheeks.

Sarah lifted her hands to clasp his strong sun-tanned wrists. 'Carlos . . . there's something I must ask you. Did you . . . was there ever anything between you and Kristen?'

'Kristen?' For a moment he looked blank. 'Do you mean Erik's wife?'

She nodded.

'No . . . never. What makes you ask?'

'The morning we met you out riding . . . perhaps you don't remember . . .'

'On the contrary, I remember it clearly. You look very attractive on horseback. I wished you had been my companion instead of hers. What made you think there was something between us? Did Kristen imply that there was?'

'It was more than an implication. She accused you of trying to persuade her to be unfaithful to Erik.'

'I see. That explains a great deal. Well, I don't like defaming any member of your sex, but in the circumstances I feel justified in telling you that Kristen's infidelities have long been common gossip. She has amused herself with numerous men while Erik studied Andalusian bird life. In my case it may be she thought to exchange a middle-aged ornithol-ogist for someone she wrongly assumed to be a playboy and jet-setter. You have my word there was never anything between us . . . except in her imagination.'

'You did tell her she looked terrific just before she introduced us.'

'I often compliment women. Why not? Kristen was looking good that night. But the reason I came over to speak to her was to be introduced to you. No doubt she guessed that and was piqued. Whatever she told you was probably prompted by a desire to kick me in the teeth for not succumbing to her rather obvious charms. But I prefer more subtle lures.'

At this point his horse began to feel left out. Nudging Carlos's shoulder and blowing a warm gust of breath down Sarah's arm, the Arab reminded them of his presence.

He also reminded Sarah that very soon now her small charge would be waking up.

'I must get back to the house. Paula will be justifiably cross if Alexander wakes her because I'm not there!' she exclaimed.

'Amparo will see to him if he starts crying. Paula is going to have to find herself another nanny. My need is greater than Alexander's,' said Carlos.

'Yes, but meanwhile I am responsible for him.'

'All right, we'll go back.'

Picking her up as easily as he had the last time they were on this beach together, he tossed her into the saddle and swung himself up behind her.

It was a dream-like experience to ride through the golden morning with Carlos's arms encircling her and his feet in the stirrups so that her legs were supported by his long muscular thighs. The three of them, horse and riders, seemed in perfect harmony. Sarah felt happiness coursing through her like the bubbles in a glass of champagne.

When a breeze ruffled the Arab's mane and lifted her hair from her nape, Carlos bent and pressed his warm lips to the curve between her neck and shoulder.

'The morning I came to see you in Albion Street, you told me you couldn't remember why you had liked me. Is your memory any better this morning?' he asked, with a smile in his voice.

Sarah leaned back against his chest and began to

tell him why she loved him; knowing there were many reasons she had yet to discover, and that the sum of her love was something she would only know in the far distant future, after a lifetime of loving him.

Coming in April
Harlequin Category Romance Specials!

Look for six new and exciting titles from this mix of two genres.

4 Regencies—lighthearted romances set in England's Regency period (1811-1820)

2 Gothics—romance plus suspense, drama and adventure

Regencies

Daughters Four by Dixie Lee McKeone
She set out to matchmake for her sister, but reckoned without the Earl of Beresford's devilish sense of humor.

Contrary Lovers by Clarice Peters
A secret marriage contract bound her to the most interfering man she'd ever met!

Miss Dalrymple's Virtue by Margaret Westhaven
She needed a wealthy patron—and set out to buy one with the only thing she had of value....

The Parson's Pleasure by Patricia Wynn
Fate was cruel, showing her the ideal man, then making it impossible for her to have him....

Gothics

Shadow over Bright Star by Irene M. Pascoe
Did he want her shares to the silver mine, her love—or her life?

Secret at Orient Point by Patricia Werner
They seemed destined for tragedy despite the attraction between them....

CAT88A-1

Harlequin Intrigue
Adopts a New Cover Story!

**We are proud to present to you
the new Harlequin Intrigue cover design.**

Look for two exciting new stories each month, which mix a contemporary, sophisticated romance with the surprising twists and turns of a puzzler . . . romance with "something more."

PAMELA BROWNING

...is fireworks on the green at the Fourth of July and prayers said around the Thanksgiving table. It is the dream of freedom realized in thousands of small towns across this great nation.

But mostly, the Heartland is its people. People who care about and help one another. People who cherish traditional values and give to their children the greatest gift, the gift of love.

American Romance presents HEARTLAND, an emotional trilogy about people whose memories, hopes and dreams are bound up in the acres they farm.

HEARTLAND...the story of America.

Don't miss these heartfelt stories: American Romance #237 SIMPLE GIFTS (March), #241 FLY AWAY (April), and #245 HARVEST HOME (May).

CAROLE MORTIMER

JUST ONE NIGHT

Hawk Sinclair—Texas millionaire and owner of the exclusive
Sinclair hotels, determined to protect his son's inheritance.
Leonie Spencer—desperate to protect her sister's happiness.

They were together for just one night.
The night their daughter was conceived.

Blackmail, kidnapping and attempted murder add suspense
to passion in this exciting bestseller.

The success story of Carole Mortimer continues with *Just
One Night*, a captivating romance from the author of the
bestselling novels, *Gypsy* and *Merlyn's Magic*.

**Available in March
wherever paperbacks are sold.**

WTCH-1